Hanigm
10a

THE LAST ROMANTIC

He signed it "Yours, with sensuous desire, Anon." On the other hand, that "sensuous desire" might, very probably would, give her the wrong idea. He crossed out "sensuous desire" and placed the letter under his pillow. He would not send it right away. Tantalize her with his delay. Besides, it needed a bit of editing here and there. Change a word here, a phrase there. He was striving for perfection. When it came to love letters, he was a perfectionist.

"Constance C. Greene is one of the best."
—*Philadelphia Inquirer*

"A wry and human story that beautifully captures the confusions of growing up." —*School Library Journal*

The Love Letters
— of —
J. Timothy Owen

Constance C. Greene

A Harper Keypoint Book

Library of Congress Cataloging-in-Publication Data
Greene, Constance C.
  The love letters of J. Timothy Owen.

  Summary: Sixteen-year-old Tim thinks he has found
the ultimate romantic courtship when he starts
sending his secret love anonymous copies of the
world's greatest love letters, but he gets unexpected
results.
  [1. Courtship—Fiction] I. Title.
PZ7.G8287Lo 1986   [Fic]   85-45846
ISBN 0-06-022156-9
ISBN 0-06-022157-7 (lib. bdg.)
ISBN 0-694-05621-9 (pbk.)

First Harper Keypoint edition, 1988.
Harper Keypoint books are published by
Harper & Row, Publishers, Inc.

For Philip and Lucia, readers and writers
of love letters nonpareil, with love and thanks.

Chapter 1

He kept the motor going as he leaned on the mower and covertly studied the girl. She was baby-sitting the kids next door, monsters all. He wanted to let her know he was on her side, was offering up a few prayers, maybe even a novena or two, for her health and safety. But how? He didn't want her to think he was a complete wacko.

He wore his thick, tan hair long over his high forehead to conceal its depth and width, a suitable repository for his many weird thoughts. His Adam's apple, big enough to fend for itself, was a good prop, and his glasses, purchased at Woolworth's—thick, professorial-type glasses—completed the image he chose to present to the world at large: a slightly off-the-wall, undercover intellectual. Inside, he was a true romantic, a veritable mush of romanticism. He would die if anyone discovered his secret.

He'd already blown it once or twice. Long ago. Take third grade. He'd sent Jennifer, Jennifer of the pigeon-toes and the scraggly pigtails, five valentines. He'd gone early to school and had slipped them into the valentine box on the teacher's desk before anyone else had arrived. All five were handmade beauties signed "Guess Who?" Then he'd signed, in the left-hand corner, his name: Tim O.

Jennifer had showed and told. They'd all laughed. Tony Montaldo had led the laughter, kept it going. "Guess who? Tim O.!" was the hue and cry. Tony was a big, good-looking kid who'd sat behind him and copied his arithmetic answers because Tim was good at arithmetic.

"How's it going, Tim O.?" Tony had shouted regularly. Tony wouldn't let go. "How's it going, Tim O.?" Tim had managed to conceal his hurt as well as his anger, but it still rankled.

Then, in an excess of romantic zeal in seventh grade, he'd thrown handfuls of pebbles at the window of a girl named Karen. A habit, he'd read, of long-ago lovers, it seemed to him a wonderfully romantic thing to do. Karen's father, however, took exception. Angered, no doubt, by his interrupted TV show, as well as a cracked windowpane, he'd given chase. Through backyards and over garbage pails they'd flown, he and Karen's dad, with Tim always a little out front, spurred on by adrenaline, youth, and terror. This incident had dampened the romantic fire always burning in his insides.

Until now. He hoped they were paying her a fortune, because that's what baby-sitting those kids was worth. He knew. He'd done it. In the olden days, five years or so ago, eager for a fast buck, a bag of M&M's, and unlimited TV, he'd been available at a moment's notice. The parents of the monsters, new in town, thought him a gem. Which he was. Living next door as he did, and being big for his age (eleven at the time), and cheap, he was called on whenever they felt the need of a breath of fresh air, which was often. A flick to be seen, a quiet dinner *à deux*, the shrink to be visited, whatever. Those monsters took a toll on the old nervous system, thereby lining his pockets.

He might still be baby-sitting, if the monsters' parents hadn't one day read once too often of the abundance of child molesters. Behind every tree, every steering wheel, lurking in every bulrush. Male baby-sitters, it seemed, were particularly suspect, henceforth persona non grata. From that day forward, the parents of the monsters worked hard at avoiding Tim's eye as they led a seemingly unending procession down

3

the garden path, of tottering old ladies trailing their knitting, or girl-children fresh from their orthodontists, live sacrifices all, as the eyes and the teeth of the monsters gleamed a welcome from behind damask draperies.

What those parents didn't know, what he'd never told, was that *he'd* been the target of molestation, rather than the kids. Upon reflection, he considered himself lucky to be alive. Fortunately, he'd been a Boy Scout, and had also taken a survival course offered at the Y. Those kids had thrown some pretty heavy stuff his way. Masters at tying sophisticated knots, they also knew a multitude of ways to shut off the supply of oxygen to the brain. One memorable afternoon, the three oldest monsters had come close to trapping him in a handmade hangman's noose, with which they'd attempted to hoist him to the rafters in the garage. Thanks to his intense interest in reading all available literature concerning the renowned escape artist Houdini, Tim had wriggled free in the nick of time. Oh, how the monsters' faces had fallen; how they'd wept, the only time they'd done so, as he paraded before them, alive, victorious.

He sighed now, contemplating the girl from afar. Her cheekbones were a work of art. Her legs, long as a stork's and considerably more symmetrical, were comely, enticing. Her mouth was a bright-red beacon, luring him onto the shoals. A natural beauty—one of few—her name, he happened to know, was Sophie. She was a sophomore and played oboe in the school band.

"Cut it out, Benjy!" he heard her holler from the neighbors' lawn. Little did she know that one word of protest acted like the proverbial red flag to Benjy. His blood, always on the simmer, reached a full, rolling boil, and his killer instincts, located close to his skin, emerged, fully developed. The other monsters, Tim noted, were out of sight, probably scouting around for some kindling to get a good blaze going in the master bedroom, a room without a fireplace.

"Tim!" His mother's voice, calling from the house, had a high, clear ring to it. She seemed to get nervous when she saw him standing still, doing nothing. She'd been on edge since his thirteenth birthday, when he'd become a full-fledged teenager. The day he'd hit thirteen, she'd started to go to pieces. Now that he was sixteen, she was still going downhill. He raised a hand to show her he'd heard and bent over the mower, pretending its motor had conked out and he was doing his best to get it going again. People were too uptight these days, he reflected, peering through his hair for a better look at The Girl. (Even though he knew her name was Sophie, in his head he called her The Girl.)

Uptight about everything—teenagers, child molesters, security systems, triple locks, guard dogs, you name it.

"Tim, are you almost finished? I need some help." His mother had gone into the antique business in an effort to keep busy, make some money, and allay her anxieties—anxieties about him, his father, cholesterol, cellulite, anorexia, bulimia, the world in general, to say nothing of nuclear waste. She collected things—willowware, fans, old clothes, whirligigs—Americana in all forms. Once, in an effort to re-create a cabin in the woods, circa 1845, she'd draped the TV set in an old quilt, attempting to disguise it. She was queer for weather vanes, old baskets, Shaker pegboards. If it was art deco, she snapped it up. When she wasn't going to auctions, she was ravaging tag sales in the hope of flushing out an unsigned Picasso, or some ancient portrait of Abraham Lincoln done by an itinerant artist on oilcloth. It was the oilcloth that pushed up the price.

Then there was that story on the six-o'clock news, of an outrageously ugly candy dish, bought at a tag sale for two bucks and sold at an auction in a high five-figure bracket after said candy dish was found to have been made by some canny Frenchman smart enough to have turned out only two such outrageously ugly candy dishes, the other being prominently displayed in the Louvre. Tim's mother thrived on such

6

stories and woke each morning, renewed, certain that today would be her day in the sun.

"Yeah, Ma, coming!"

A rustling in the bushes and a spate of giggles told him he was not alone. He glimpsed a couple of straw-colored heads and some bare flesh. The monsters were deploying their forces.

He got the mower going, revved the engine, and aimed it at the clump of bushes. Maybe he could wipe out the lot of them in one fell swoop. Mow 'em down, to coin a phrase.

"Coming for you!" he roared as he and his mower advanced noisily. The bushes trembled as if caught in a typhoon, but were not sundered. He kept on going, growing a little apprehensive, even considered backing down, thereby losing face. He didn't fancy having a murder rap hung on him.

With seconds to spare, the bushes parted, spewing three scantily clad bodies topped by three straw-colored heads, all screaming with glee and the excitement of bloodletting, even if the blood turned out to be their own.

Then a commotion next door silenced even the monsters, and they watched as the girl wrestled Benjy to the ground and sat on him. For that alone, he could've kissed her. For not only was she beautiful, she was also strong.

Chapter 2

Before his mother would allow him to go next door to baby-sit, she had insisted on demonstrating to him the fine art of diapering a baby, as there seemed to be quite a few babies among the tribe of monsters. Moreover, most of them appeared to be wearing diapers. Either that or large, billowing behinds ran in their family. Like baldness. Or blue eyes. The monsters' mother revealed she had read all the books on child rearing and was against forced toilet training.

"When they're ready," she said piously, "they will let me know." In the meantime, the behinds got bigger and soggier, and the air in the monsters' house got pretty steamy on a hot summer's day.

Using an ancient diaper and Tim's scraggly old teddy bear, which she somewhat sheepishly brought from its hiding place for use in her diapering demo, his mother had said in her precise way, "You fold it with the thickness in front if it's a boy baby, Tim, and with the thickness in back if it's a girl."

So it was he learned the facts of life, sort of.

He liked little kids. Maybe he'd have some of his own when he was thirty, and rich. Or forty, and richer. One of his friends' fathers was pushing sixty. When the father showed up at school on occasion, some smart ass always said, "Who's the old geezer?" It didn't seem to bother his friend, and presumably the old geezer never heard.

He heard the girl calling the monsters home to roost. Her voice sounded thin and strained and anxious, probably wondering what she'd do with them once they got there, or, if they didn't show, how she'd explain their absence to their parents.

He turned off the mower, conserving gas. His mother had gone inside, no doubt to mull over the merits of collecting Oriental rugs as opposed to old baseball cards.

The monsters, flushed fresh from the shrubbery, arranged themselves in a tight circle at his feet, ready to gnaw on his ankles if need be. He thought he heard a whirring sound, the tiny, tinny sound of their collective brains plotting his immediate demise. Only their eyes moved, eyes as big and as flat as silver dollars. They lifted their angelic faces to him, as flowers lift theirs to the sun. What a scene. The whirring sound continued. Either it was their brains working overtime or a rattlesnake off course. Hard to say which he feared most.

"So why don't you guys pack it in, go home, and put on the feed bag? The baby-sitter's probably got a treat for you." The eyes widened, the mouths remained clamped shut. They gave him the silent treatment, figuring it would turn him to jelly, as it had so many others.

Sometimes the sudden move won the Cracker Jacks. "You!" he snapped, leveling a grass-green finger at the biggest monster, who wore cutoffs and a sneer. "You're the general!"

Who could resist that? Everybody wants to be the general, right?

"You're the pilot," he told the girl. "And you're the adjutant," he addressed the smallest monster.

It was all in the choice of words; that and the authoritative snap with which they left his mouth. That took care of the lot. Keep moving, keep talking. At least he had their complete attention.

"Ready, march!" he bellowed, and, miracle of miracles, they obeyed. Revving the engine once more, he pushed the mower before him like a Sherman tank, and goose-stepped across the yard with the troops

10

following on his heels. If it works, don't knock it, was his slogan for the day.

When they reached the back door of the monsters' house, he turned off the mower and opened the screen door. He marched inside, and they followed, lambs being led to the slaughter.

Benjy lay on the floor supporting his head in his cupped hands. The TV set dithered and spouted weird noises and bright lights and screams of greed from the contestants trying for a new refrigerator.

The baby-sitter had gone. Had she, perhaps, bolted, unable to stand the gaff? Or was she even now suspended from a homemade hangman's noose in the garage, heels dangling in the murky air?

Neither. He was relieved to hear a pounding on the bathroom door, indicating her presence within.

"You little weasel!" he snarled at Benjy, who smiled vacantly around the edges of his grimy paws and continued to watch the carnage on the small screen. He went to the bathroom door and turned the knob. Locked. No key in sight.

"Let her out before I break both your legs," he said. Wordlessly, the general in the cutoffs rummaged under the rug and brought forth a key.

"He's so dumb he always puts it in exactly the same place," the general explained.

The key fitted the lock; he turned it and the door

swung open. The girl sat on the edge of the bathtub chewing a fingernail.

She jumped to her feet, pale with rage. "That's the first and last time I baby-sit in this hellhole!" she cried. "I don't care if they pay me ten bucks an hour. You couldn't drag me in here again. Who are you?" She narrowed her eyes at him. "Are you in this, too?" She clenched her fists and he prepared to duck. "Let me go or I'll scream. I'll scream bloody murder." He didn't doubt it.

"I'm . . . " he began, but she wasn't listening.

"I have a brown belt in karate!" she shouted. "You lay a finger on me and I'll put you on your back just like that!"

He was not averse to the idea of her putting him on his back but, at the moment, he wanted to comfort her. His mouth opened and closed like a fish coming up for air. She started to edge past him. He was careful not to touch her. The monsters lined up, watching, listening, intrigued by this real-life drama.

"You lay a hand on me and you'll regret it," the girl said. He made himself concave as she sidestepped him, so no part of him would touch her as she made her escape. How could she know he was a knight in shining armor, a courtier, a vagabond lover? He felt like breaking into song, if only he could carry a tune. He wished for a Royal Canadian Mountie's red coat or a snow-white charger to carry him into battle so he could slay all the dragons in the kingdom for his fair maiden.

"Buzz off!" hissed the fair maiden, eyes shooting sparks.

The sound of the family car limping into the drive brought all hands around. The silver-dollar eyes darted hither and yon in a search-and-destroy mission of all evidence.

"There you are, my darlings!" the monsters' mother cried, refreshed by her hiatus. She stopped short, her mouth an O of astonishment. "Why, Tim, what on earth are you doing here? You know we don't allow boys in the house while we're not home, dear," she turned to the girl. "That's against the rules." The monsters lowered their eyes, stunned into silence. They hadn't known there were any rules.

"We won't stand for any teenage hanky-panky here," the mother announced, gathering her chicks under her wings, two to a wing. The girl shook her head as if she'd just been dealt a severe blow to her solar plexus. Tim admired her solar plexus, as well as the way her muscles moved under her luscious skin, and wished for a set of muscles nearly as nice.

"I never saw him before in my life," the girl snapped.

She passed him almost every day of her life, going

13

in and out of the science lab. He must have a forgettable face, he thought sadly.

"I was locked in the bathroom and, all of a sudden,
he burst in."

Had he burst? He'd thought he was doing her a
favor.

"If there's a problem here, I'm sure it can be worked
out." The monsters' mother, eminently reasonable and
open to suggestion, stroked her childrens' heads tenderly as they gazed, glassy-eyed, at their filthy feet.

Outside, the car horn blasted. The monsters' dad
was waiting, no doubt, to drive the baby-sitter home.

"Poor Daddy is losing his patience." The mother
opened her purse and peered inside. "I only have a
five-dollar bill," she said. "Will that be all right?"

"No," said the girl. He admired very much the way
she stated this simple fact. "No, you owe me for four
hours, at two dollars an hour. That's eight dollars,
without a tip," she said firmly.

"Yes, how stupid of me. You take the five and my
husband will give you the rest. Thank you, dear. I'll
be in touch."

"She sat on my stomach," Benjy chirped.

"Oh, my. Is that true? Did you sit on my baby's
stomach?"

"Yeah," the girl said. "And he locked me in the
bathroom."

"Oh, Benjy! Not again!" The mother sounded as if she might cry.

"Plus, he's no baby." The girl tucked the fiver in her pocket. "In some ancient cultures, he'd be out in the fields picking rice. So long kids, don't eat any poisonous mushrooms." She grinned suddenly, and Tim fell in love all over again.

Chapter 3

"Tim, be very careful with this one, will you? It's full of practically irreplaceable china." His mother stood over him, supervising. She was a born supervisor. She had bought a bunch of stuff from someone's attic, and he was helping her sort it. His father was coming for dinner. With Joy. Joy lived next door to his father in his new condo. They were just friends, his mother said. Joy was a computer programmer who had just moved in and was newly divorced herself. Joy ate TV dinners, his father said, laughing. His mother was a pushover for hungry people. "Bring her for dinner, why don't you?" she'd said. Tim had expected a middle-aged lady wearing sensible shoes and a three-piece suit, but Joy had been thin and thirty-two, and something of an airhead, he'd thought. He had noticed his mother and father got along much better now than when they had been married. And when Joy was there, all was sweetness and light at the dinner table, the four of them jabbering away like old sorority buddies.

"Whadya mean, practically irreplaceable? Either it's irreplaceable or it's not," he said.

"Tim, I have absolutely no time to argue with you now. I told Kev I'd have the stuff unpacked when he got here, to give him a chance to look it over. And he'll be here in half an hour. Or an hour. Whichever's soonest." His mother sometimes delivered lines in a way that, if you didn't know her, might make you think she was an airhead, too. Far from the case. She was some smart cookie.

Kev was his mother's partner in the antique shop. He was thirty-seven and gorgeous. Or so Tim's mother thought.

"Isn't he gorgeous?" was the first thing she'd said after Kev had left that first night he showed up at the house. "Isn't he the most gorgeous thing you ever saw?"

"You want a straight answer?" was what he'd said to that. But his mother had been occupied with other things and hadn't answered.

"Look at this!" she cried now. "Will you just look at this!"

He went over to see what all the excitement was about.

"It looks like an old trunk to me," he said.

"It *is* an old trunk. See what's inside. Why, they must've been here for ages. More than a hundred years, I'll bet. Maybe more than that."

His mother's eyes shone. Nothing turned her on like the mention of age, as long as it wasn't her own. She got all hot and bothered when she talked about the age of a piece of furniture, or a picture, or anything she collected. "It has some age to it," she always said when trying to justify what seemed to him an outrageously high price for some piece of old junk.

Now, carefully, tenderly, she lifted from the trunk's bottom a pile of tattered paper tied with a pale ribbon. "They're old letters," she said softly. "Just look, Tim. They're tied with this beautiful ribbon. I'll bet they're love letters. What do you want to bet? Otherwise, why would they have been saved?" She began to untie the ribbon and it fell apart in her hand, sending the letters drifting to the ground like the last leaves of autumn.

"I told you!" his mother crowed. "Why, the ribbon was so old it just disintegrated. Isn't that marvelous?"

"Maybe they're letters from George Washington to old Martha from Valley Forge," he suggested. "Or from Abe Lincoln to John Wilkes Booth telling him he was a bad actor." He liked that one.

"I think I hear Kev. Back in a minute." His mother flew off in the new, girlish way she'd had since the advent of Kev into her life.

He stayed where he was, his imagination fired by finding the old letters. Even if they weren't love letters, they were still interesting simply because they were old. And if they turned out to speak words of love, it would be all right to read them, because all the lovers concerned must be long gone.

On his hands and knees, he crawled around, gathering up the letters. He glanced at one now and then. There were no envelopes, simply musty-smelling pieces of paper covered, for the most part, in spidery, slanted handwriting. The same person must have written them all, he thought.

"My dearest darling," one began, and he hastily looked away, as if he'd intruded on something very personal. My dearest darling. Nobody talked like that. Not anymore they didn't. But what did you say after openers like that?

"I carry with me your dear face," the letter went on, and, entranced, he settled down to read it all. "I have no need of perfumed remembrances. I smell your scent, it is with me all the day and night, sweeter than any flower." Then the guy had to blow it all by telling a long, boring story about how the locks on the Erie Canal had gotten stuck and had made him late in his arrival in Buffalo. What a turkey. The letter was signed "Thine, until Death doth part us." The letter writer's name was Willie.

"Kev's here, Tim." His mother stood there, beaming, presenting Kev to him like a present wrapped in shiny paper and tied with a big bow. "Hi, fella," Kev said, as if he were a dog. Kev always called him "fella." He personally had known three dogs called Fella. Was Kev trying to tell him something?

He got up off the floor, lifted a hand in greeting, and put the letters back into the trunk.

Thine, until Death doth part us. Heavy, really heavy. But eye-catching. Capital D for Death. He'd have to remember that. Maybe he could use it sometime. The last letter he'd written had been a thank-you note to his grandparents after Christmas for a ten-dollar check they'd sent. They still thought ten bucks was a fortune. They'd told him not to spend it all in one place. Probably they thought he would use the money to take a trip to Vegas, play the slots, buy the show girls champagne, and play chemin de fer until the sun came up.

"I think you'll like this china, Kev," his mother said. She was always trying to please this bozo, trying to make him say that something she'd bought was a real find. It made him sick, the way she tried to please

Kev. And Kev was very picky. Compared to Kev, Tim's father was a piece of cake.

"Umm." Kev inspected the china. "Chip here." With his thumb Kev traced the chip on a cup. That was the way Kev operated, point out the bad things straight off, ignore the good. The china looked OK to Tim, although, perhaps, not museum quality. They were always talking about stuff being "museum quality." If it was museum quality, why wasn't it in a museum?

Kev came over to where he was kneeling by the trunk.

"What's that?" Kev looked inside the trunk.

"Letters."

"We found a pile of old letters in the trunk," his mother said. "Tim's intrigued."

"Maybe they're worth something," Kev said, hunkering down, picking up the pile, thumbing through it. "You never know."

He wanted to say, "Hands off. They're mine!" and was wise enough to keep quiet.

"They're only valuable if they're written by famous people," he said quickly. He didn't want Kev kibitzing. Those letters were his, his and his mother's. He didn't want Kev sticking his nose in where he wasn't wanted. Besides, Kev would only make fun of them. "I have to split," he said, getting up. "Got a science project to finish."

21

"Oh, it's Pasteur at work, is it?" Kev flashed one of his famous grins, trying to be friends. No such luck, Kev. You have no idea of what a jerk you are. Why don't you take your tent and silently steal away, like the poet said? Kev had a bright-orange tent he lugged around with him in an effort to establish himself as a lover of the great outdoors. Tim was willing to bet Kev never pitched that tent very far away from hot running water and a diner whose parking lot was loaded with trucks, their drivers inside shoveling down excellent chow. Kev had suggested they go camping together, just the two of them. His mother thought that a wonderful idea. He told Kev, truthfully, about his fear of snakes and porcupines. Kev laughed until he choked and had to be pounded on the back. The orange tent was stowed in their garage for safekeeping, waiting for the call of the wild to beckon once again.

He pocketed the letters surreptitiously as his mother showed Kev a box of old books she'd picked up at a tag sale.

"I don't suppose there are any first editions?" Kev asked, already bored. He had the attention span of a two-year-old, Kev did. He'd invested some money in the antique shop, which was housed in a run-down building at the end of an alley off the main street in town. The landlord spent his winters in the Bahamas and gave them a special price if they signed a year's lease.

"A special high price," his father had said when told of the arrangement. But it wasn't any of his father's business what his mother chose to do. Not anymore it wasn't.

"I hope you didn't pay more than a couple of bucks for these." Kev inspected the books with a small sneer on his face. "They're a mess. You have to be more selective, Maddy, when you buy. The condition of these is deplorable." Kev fingered a book with a broken spine, its pages stained and torn. "You might as well get rid of this one. Along with all the others. They smell, too."

"Old books always smell," Tim's mother said. "It's part of their charm." He knew that, sooner or later, she'd dump this guy. The only thing he couldn't figure was why she put up with him in the first place.

"Maybe it is for you," Kev said, winking elaborately at him, "but count me out."

"Fine with me," Tim said. They both looked at him. "What's fine with you?" his mother asked.

"Kev said 'count me out,' and I was just saying that was fine with me," he answered lamely. Talk about putting the quietus on a conversation. He was an ace.

"Will you come out to the garage for a minute, Kev?" his mother said hastily. "I've got a ladder-back chair I think might, just might, be original Shaker."

They left him. He was ashamed of what he'd said to Kev. Not because he didn't mean it, but because he knew it had hurt his mother. She wanted them to be buddies, him and Kev.

The books, he noticed, were covered with a thick layer of dust. He couldn't read any of the titles. He blew vigorously, and the dust rose to clog his nose and throat. Serves me right, he thought, wheezing, patting the books, feeling sorry for them. Poor things. They were unwanted, neglected, and devastated by age and lack of care. Now that the dust had settled, he could see there were some old medical books, a set of Britannica volumes from 1911, as well as novels and books of poetry. Most of the books looked so frail he was afraid they'd fall apart if he picked them up.

One Hundred of the World's Best Love Letters. That's what the title of the book was. Amazed at the co-incidence, he put one finger gently on the book, as if to separate it from the others. Who decided which letters were the best? He picked it up gingerly and weighed it in his hand. It was slender, almost weight-less. Probably there weren't that many great love let-ters around. He opened it to the table of contents. Beau Brummell, Edgar Allan Poe, Lord Byron, and to his astonishment, Benjamin Franklin. He'd seen plenty of pictures of old Ben Franklin, and he sure didn't look like the kind of guy who'd write any love letters. Or the kind of guy anybody would be in love with.

He took the book of love letters up to his room and tossed it on his bed. Then he took the packet of letters from his pocket and stuck it under his pillow. Sometimes he memorized poetry or committed passages or phrases that caught his fancy to memory, thinking he might have use for them in some future, more exotic existence. He was a collector, too, though not of Americana. Of words, words that brought him to the brink of some nameless, tearing emotion, words that moved or touched him, or made him laugh. Words it never would have occurred to him to put together. Or phrases that struck such a chord in him as to render him speechless, breathless, dazzled by the author's prescience and sensitivity. A "voice like jewels dropped into a satin bag." A line from a poem. Did such a voice exist? He certainly hoped so. Words that said what he'd been thinking and feeling but that he hadn't had the power to articulate.

"You stinketh in God's nostrils," he'd read somewhere recently. Worth remembering.

The telephone rang. When he picked it up, a voice said, "Hello, fool."

It was Patrick. Try and call him Pat and see where

that got you. "Hello, Pat," he said back. Patrick's heavy breathing flooded the line.

"I was only teasing," he said. "You want to hear a love letter written by Benjamin Franklin?"

Patrick said, "Who's she?"

"My mother bought a bunch of old books and there's this one called *One Hundred of the World's Best Love Letters*," he told Patrick. "I'm really getting into it. Getting ideas."

"Who would you write a love letter *to?*" said Patrick, scoring a point.

"Shirley Temple? I'm thinking along those lines."

Patrick snorted. "She's old enough to be your grandmother."

"Hey, I saw her last week in *Little Miss Marker* and she was looking good," he said. "A little young, maybe, six or seven, along there, but still hanging in there."

"Yeah, they probably made that movie about fifty-five years ago," Patrick said.

"Whoa! Hold it. You just shot me down in flames. But don't worry, I'll come up with somebody."

"How about Lauren Bacall?" Patrick said. "She's hot stuff."

"I think she's dead. Yeah, I'm almost positive she's dead."

"You're crazy. She's as alive as you or me."

"You know a girl named Sophie?" he let slip, not having planned to mention her name.

"Sophie? You mean Giraffe? That's what they call her, 'Giraffe,' on account of her legs. That the Sophie you mean?"

"I don't know about that," he said, offended by Patrick's description. "I didn't notice her legs," he lied.

"Oh, well, if you didn't notice her legs, you and me are talking about two different Sophies. The one I'm talking about has legs so long they call her Giraffe, like I said."

"I have to split," he said, sorry he'd brought up her name at all.

"Yeah, well, I'll run a dossier on Lauren Bacall. If she's not dead, she might be your man. To write a love letter to, I mean. Except there's one thing."

"What's that?"

"Humphrey Bogart. He might not like it. *Ciao.*" And Patrick hung up on him, just in time.

Chapter 4

"I'm funny that way." Joy wrinkled her nose at the company at large. They had polished off the salad and were waiting for dessert. "I like all new. Give me new stuff any day."

"Surely you jest, madam." Kev had drunk a lot of wine and, as usual, when tiddly, he took on airs.

"Dear Madam," Kev pontificated, winding up for one of Shakespeare's sonnets, perhaps. Fortunately, the timer on the stove went off, and his mother dashed to snatch the soufflé from the oven before it fell. His father, slightly hard of hearing, smiled and drummed his fingers on the table, the scent of chocolate making him happy.

"Old is in, new is out," Kev proclaimed, taking another slug of the best burgundy Gallo had to offer.

"If I ever have a house," Joy continued, as if Kev

hadn't spoken, thereby winning points with Tim, if no one else, "I want all white. Rugs, couches, chairs, drapes, the works. All white."

His mother's hearing, however, was acute. She came from the kitchen bearing the soufflé before her and set it down gently and said, "Drape is a verb, Joy, not a noun. You shouldn't say 'drape' when you mean curtains or draperies." His mother had been a teacher of sixth-grade English, when fresh from college, and had often said there were some things one never gets over. Being an English teacher was high on the list.

"Joy?" His mother dipped her spoon into the soufflé. The spoon sank without whisper, and she passed the first portion to Joy, who sat, rigid and red-faced, no doubt justly irritated at being treated like a sixth grader.

"Oh, I couldn't!" Joy cried. "I have to watch my figure."

They were all too busy watching the soufflé serving to comment on this obvious ploy. When everyone had been served, they dug in. Joy scanned the diners, and, when she saw that no one was giving her the time of day, she dug in, too.

"This is good, Maddy," his father said. "I always did like your chocolate the best."

His father's hair had gone quite gray, and he'd grown sideburns since his last visit.

"I like your burns, Dad," he said.

29

His father gave him a look. "I feel as if someone's following me," his father said, "and all I know is, he must be a very hairy gent because all I can see of him is his hair." One thing about his father, he knew how to laugh at himself, a very endearing characteristic.

"I think he looks wonderful," Joy said. "They make him look so much younger. Don't you think?"

His father flushed and, to change the subject, Tim said, "You playing any tennis lately, Dad?" They often played tennis together on weekends, he and his father. Sometimes his mother joined them with a friend, and they played doubles. None of them was terribly good but they had fun together.

"Didn't I tell you? I've taken up golf." His father smiled. "Joy's idea. She has a ten handicap." Tim didn't know much about golf but he knew a ten handicap was good.

"Oh, and he's pretty good at it, too!" Joy exclaimed. He wondered if she ever spoke in a quiet voice. He found her vivacity somewhat daunting.

"For a beginner," Joy went on, turning from one to the other of them, making sure they were all in on it, "he's really quite good."

"If you want to play a couple of sets, Dad, I'm available," he said.

"Thanks, Tim, I'd like that."

Kev scraped his spoon against his empty dessert

plate and said, "Speaking of tennis, seconds anyone?"

Kev was such an ass. There was no excuse for anyone being such a super ass.

"Tim." Joy laid a hand on his arm. "If you'd like to join us for golf, we'd love to have you. Wouldn't we?" She turned to his father, who happened to be talking to his mother, giving her his full attention. This was a strange group, he thought. His parents, his mother's business partner and sometime boyfriend, his father's next-door neighbor and sometime girlfriend, and himself, sixteen years old with nothing to show for it.

He looked down at Joy's hand, which still rested on his arm, for lack of anything better to do. Kev was involved in getting up all traces of chocolate soufflé without actually picking up his plate and licking it.

Joy's fingers, he noticed, were laden with diamond rings, at least three of them. Seeing him looking at her rings, Joy said, "My mother once told me, 'Joy, you have diamond hands. Don't settle for rhinestones.' "

There wasn't a whole lot to be said to that. His father cleared his throat noisily. Tim said, "Thanks, Joy, I wouldn't mind taking up golf someday. I watch a lot of the tournaments on TV, and it looks like fun. Well, of course, those guys are pros. They can make anything look like fun."

Kev never had liked being left out of a conversa-

31

tion. "You find anything worthwhile in that bundle of old letters from the trunk?" he asked, somewhat truculently.

"Tim and I found a pile of old love letters in a trunk I picked up at auction," his mother explained. "We're quite fascinated by them, by the whole idea of finding something so old, so personal, so revealing of the people who wrote them. And who all are dead."

"How old are they?" his father asked.

"I haven't really checked them out that carefully yet," he said, embarrassed at Kev's bringing up the subject. He had wanted to keep them to himself for a while, until he had a chance to go over them carefully. "Some are dated, but not all. Some of them go back maybe a hundred years, maybe more."

"What fun! I'd love to see them sometime, Tim," Joy said. As she spoke, she held her hand high and watched the play of light on her diamonds.

"The language gets pretty flowery," he said, laughing.

"I guess people don't write love letters anymore," his father said.

"You got me. Nobody ever wrote me one, that's for sure," he said.

Joy put in her two cents. "Oh, I've had two or three in my day, and I'm not through yet!" she said playfully. She turned from him to his father in a manner he thought could best be described as coquettish.

"All right if I clear now, Mom?" he asked, eager to escape.

"Leave it, Tim. Kev will help. I know you have homework. Good night, darling."

He was the only one his mother still called 'darling.' He liked it when she called him that. She used to call his father 'darling,' but no more.

"Good night, Dad, Joy, Kev." He kissed his mother and nodded to Kev, who was sulking conspicuously. Kev didn't like doing household chores. And with all that soufflé inside him, he might have a hard time managing.

"Don't forget the golf, Tim," Joy said. "Maybe we'll do it this Saturday, if the weather's good. Does that sound all right? We could hit a few balls at the practice range."

"Fine," he agreed. That would be great.

Too bad Joy's parents hadn't had her teeth fixed when she was a kid. She had an overbite that made her resemble a chipmunk when she smiled. Too late now. It occurred to him, as he trudged upstairs, that Kev and Joy would make an excellent team. A magic love potion might be the answer. Whip one up and give them each a shot, and they'd fall into each other's arms and take off, arm in arm, into the sunset.

Talk about killing two birds with one stone!

Chapter 5

The name Sophie jumped out at him from the page.

"Come, Sophie, that I may torture your unjust heart, that I on my side may be merciless toward you."

This was one of the world's best love letters, written by Jean-Jacques Rousseau to the Countess Sophie d'Houdetout in June, 1757. His mother would flip. That really had some age to it, all right. The letter was talking to him, trying to tell him something, he thought, excited by its endless possibilities. A brief biography stated that Rousseau was a pioneer of the Romantic movement as well as a preacher of the return-to-nature creed. Wow. Even as far back as then they were returning to nature, and all along he thought his parents' generation had invented it.

Right on, Rousseau. Probably Rousseau, or J.J. as

his friends undoubtedly called him, had a bright-orange tent just like Kev's, which he and the Countess Sophie lugged into the woods for a little hanky-panky under the stars.

"Why should I spare you whilst you rob me of reason, of honour, of life?" the letter continued. "Ah, much less cruel would you have been if you had driven a dagger into my heart instead of the fateful weapon which kills me! How often did you not say to me in the grove by the waterfall, 'You are the most tender lover that I can imagine; no, never did a man love like you!'"

The Countess Sophie did all right on her own, he thought, entranced. She knew how to sock it to old Rousseau.

"Ah, Sophie, I beseech you, do not be ashamed of a friend whom you once favored. Am I not your property? Have you not taken possession of me?"

Ah, Sophie, give me a break.

There was lots more.

"What! Your touching eyes will never droop again before my glances with that sweet shame, which so intoxicated me with sensuous desire? I am never more to feel that heavenly shudder, that maddening devouring fire, which quicker than lightning . . . oh, inexpressible moment! What heart, what god could have experienced you and resisted?"

End of letter.

No two ways about it. That J.J. Rousseau had a way with words. Where was the Count, old Sophie's husband? It made you stop and think. Suppose the Count steamed open the envelope and got a load of what was going on? The fur would fly. The Count would probably figure out that the Countess Sophie hadn't been wearing her chastity belt like she was supposed to while the Count was off to battle, suited up in his armor, fighting whoever the enemy happened to be that week.

Pretty steamy stuff.

He went through the table of contents and noted there were very few of the world's best love letters written by women. Madame du Barry, of course, had dashed off a couple. But Madame du Barry was a tiger, a hot-blooded lady from all reports, who had been Louis XV's mistress and had managed to get herself beheaded during the French Revolution.

Then there was always Elizabeth Barrett Browning, some of whose love letters were in the book. A poet by trade, she wrote quite a lot of love letters to, of all people, her husband! He was Robert Browning. They were both poets, as a matter of fact, and they sent those old love letters flying back and forth. They must've traveled a lot. Separately. Else why so many letters? They were the only married people whose love letters had been recorded. Weird. He preferred to read passionate letters of love written by folks embroiled in illicit romances. It was more interesting. He marveled at the information to be found in books.

Samuel Johnson stated, in the book's foreword, that a love letter was a written confession of affection in which the soul lies naked. The soul, his own especially, had always interested him. A naked soul. What would it look like? How would you recognize it if no one told you what it was? Not that you were likely to run into a naked soul just anywhere. But it would be good to know what it was if you should see one, just sort of lying there. He thought it might look like protoplasm: colorless, translucent. Or an amoeba, perhaps?

He liked to think that his soul had a character all its own, unique, different from all other souls. That was his ego bending itself out of shape, he figured. If he looked long enough, concentrated hard enough, maybe his soul might show itself. Maybe, in the deepest dark, his soul would stand up to be counted. Like a laser beam. A prick of light. That's what he secretly thought his soul would resemble. A darting pinprick of light. To him, the concept of the soul was romantic as well as religious. The soul was forever. The laser beam was now, today. But there was no reason the two might not be compatible. One was scientific, the other spiritual. Reason enough. He intended to delve into the possibilities of uniting laser beam and soul at some later date. Digging out a stubby pencil, he began to compose a love letter of his own.

"Dear Friend of my Bosom," he started out, his handwriting chicken tracking its way across the paper. That salutation he had borrowed from a letter Admiral Lord Nelson wrote to his mistress Emma, Lady Hamilton (wife of Lord Hamilton, natch), while at sea, noon, August 1805. The same year he polished off the French and the Spanish at the battle of Trafalgar. Boy, talk about an overachiever, that was Lord Nelson—Horatio by name—to a tee. He was always blasting the enemy out of the water someplace, but that didn't stop him from dashing off sweet nothings to Lady Hamilton. Lord Hamilton happened to be the British ambassador to Naples, who presumably had other things on his mind than Lady Hamilton, which is why she and Horatio got something going between them. The Admiral was a star, pure and simple. There he was, one hand on the tiller, the other on his pen, letting Emma know he had the hots for her bod. You had to give the guy credit. Not a wasted moment there. Plus, Nelson had lost an eye and an arm in battle. So, minus an eye, minus an arm, he went on fighting for his country and writing love letters to Lady Hamilton. It was like Tim's mother always said: busy people always found time to do the things that needed doing.

It struck him that almost all the letters in the book had been written by people having illicit affairs. In other words, marriage apparently put the kibosh on love. Passion. Whatever you want to call it. He was fond of the word "kibosh." Old-fashioned but apt.

He'd taught himself to type when he was nine. From the start his handwriting had been awful, practically illegible. He thought of typing the letter he wanted to write, and realized the letter's magic might be considerably diminished if he did so. No pencil, no typewriter, no word processor would do. It would have to be writ by hand. A crash course in calligraphy was indicated but he didn't have time. It had to be done, and done soon.

"Dear Friend of my Bosom" might be OK for Admiral Nelson, but somehow it struck a false note when Tim put it down on paper. Anyway, men didn't have bosoms, did they? He crossed it out and began again.

"Dearest Heart of my Heart." Those capital letters did the trick. "Dearest Heart of my Heart. I have ordered the carriage for seven."

That looked good.

Only, who drove the carriage while the lovers were trysting in the backseat? Whoever the driver was, he had better be deaf, dumb, and blind, else he might spill the beans. And where did the lovers tryst? The motels in the olden days were dirty and crowded, nothing like a Holiday Inn, of that he was certain. And no cars, whose roomy seats were perfect for a little making out. No wonder they used so many flowery words, such romantic hyperbole. They were sexually repressed. A terrible state of affairs.

"I rush to press you in my arms." That was an original. He had made it up and he was proud of it. It had the ring of authenticity. I rush to press you in my arms. Would she buy that? Watch out for overkill, he cautioned himself.

"I love you more tenderly each passing day. My soul reaches out for you." Copied. "Will you allow me to come to you this evening? My whole soul rejoices in the assurance of your love."

There it was again: soul.

He'd been taught in religious instructions that the soul was immortal. That it lived on after the body was dead. Did it? He'd never been completely convinced. After he'd made his first communion, at age seven, he remembered, his head had buzzed with the things he'd been taught, had memorized. He had asked his mother to show him exactly where his soul was located, as if it had been his appendix, his liver, or his heart. He figured it must have a place of its own, and if it didn't, it should. She told him his soul was all over, all through him, yet invisible. No one, she said, could show it to him, or touch it, see it, or take an X ray of it. It was a matter of faith, she said.

40

There had been a lot of talk of organ donors, papers to be signed saying that if you were killed your organs could be taken from your body and implanted in a living person, so that they might live on using your organs. That had appealed to him and he had decided to donate his organs, all of them, in the event of his untimely death. Along with his organs, he might donate his soul, so if one of the sick people in the world needed a soul to go on living, they could have his. He had felt very worthy, very holy, saintly, even, after making this decision. This was when he was eight. His mother had had a tough time concealing her amusement when he broached this subject to her. He had donated his soul to the organ bank and she was laughing at him! It had taken some time for him to recover from that.

"When you die, your soul will live on," his mother had told him. He hadn't believed her then, and he didn't believe her now.

"Like ghosts?" he'd asked her, and, again, he suspected her of laughing.

Did souls come in sizes? he wondered. Was his soul the same size as his father's, for instance? Was a baby's soul tiny, and did it grow along with the baby? Did fat people have fat souls and thin people thin ones? Did souls come in different colors, to match people's skins? The questions, all unanswered and perhaps unanswerable, were endless.

Souls had been very big at one time. Just from reading *One Hundred of the World's Best Love Letters* he could figure that out. Most of the letters had been written in the seventeenth and eighteenth centuries. In every letter, scarcely a line was written without mention of the soul, as if it were a living, breathing thing. The soul had certainly diminished in importance. You didn't hear people talk much about souls these days. Except for soul food. And soul kiss.

His mother tapped at the door and stuck in her head. "May I come in?" she asked.

He put down his letter and placed the book on top of it. "Sure," he said. His mother never pried, but he didn't want her to know he was writing his own love letter, half copying the masters, half original with him. Writing it to an unknown person.

She sat on the edge of his bed. "How did you think your father seemed?"

"All right," he said. "About the same."

"I thought he seemed sort of down," she said. "Not very happy."

What did she care if his father was happy or not? They were divorced, weren't they? He wanted to ask her if she still loved his father, but he figured that was none of his business. His mother usually respected his privacy, and he thought he owed her the same courtesy. She didn't delve into his personal life,

42

such as it was, and he stayed out of hers. His personal life held no secrets, anyway. Unless you called his midnight thoughts secret. Which they were, and a darn good thing, too.

"I wish he'd see someone else," his mother said. "Someone a little closer to his age."

"Joy's thirty-two. That's only fifteen years younger than Dad." What about Kev? he thought. He's seven years younger than you. Maybe you ought to find someone closer to your age, Mom. He didn't say it out loud but he'd thought about it more than once. It seemed a little undignified for her to be so much older than he was.

"That's Joy's story." His mother leaned close to him, as if she didn't want anyone to hear what she was saying, although they were alone in the room. "Take a look at that neck next time. If that's the neck of a thirty-two-year-old, I'll eat it."

"Ma! You start taking nips out of Joy's neck and you're in deep trouble!" At the idea, he burst out laughing and, after a minute, his mother joined in. They laughed until tears filled their eyes.

"Ah, Tim, what would I do without you?" his mother said. "You're a good boy. I love you."

More moved than he wanted to admit, he said, "If your own mother doesn't love you, who will?"

She hugged him.

"Ma," he said, "I've been thinking about souls. If you could see yours, what do you think it would look like?"

"A butterfly," she said, right off. "When I was little, someone, I don't remember who, told me that when I saw a butterfly, I would know it was a soul flying to heaven. I believed him. So I think that's what a soul looks like. It's as good an answer as any."

"This book of love letters is really something," he told her. "Don't you think it's amazing, finding those letters in the trunk and also finding the world's best love letters all laid out for you in a book? I mean, what a coincidence, right? Wild." He held up the book.

She nodded and headed for the door. "Is it fun? Let me see it when you're through with it, will you, Tim?"

On impulse, he asked, "Did you ever write a love letter to Dad? Or did he ever write one to you?"

"I wrote him a couple and tore them up," she said. "I was too reserved, too afraid of making a fool of myself to put down on paper what I felt for him. And your father was never good at expressing himself. A shame, really. I've had to learn to tell people how I feel about them. It didn't come naturally, Tim. It's a good thing to learn. Don't be afraid to tell someone you love how you feel. Everyone likes being loved, I think."

Her eyes took on a faraway look, as if she were seeing people and places of long ago. Then she said ruefully, "Enough of that. I got carried away."

Everyone likes being loved, his mother had said. True. And everyone loves being liked. And it was probably a good thing not to take loving, or liking either, for granted, he thought. And hard not to.

He decided to change the subject. "Mom, listen to this, will you?" He read, " 'My treasure, my dearest life and love, how can I refuse you your happiness? My whole soul rejoices in the assurances of your love and to your exertions I will trust.' " He watched her to see how she'd react.

"My heavens!" She drew her hand across her forehead, putting a strand of hair in place. "If you wrote that to anyone these days, they'd think you were a nut, wouldn't they?" She smiled at him and said, "Good night and sleep tight, Timmy," as if he were a child again.

"Night, Ma," he said. For some time after she'd gone, he thought about what she'd said about telling people you loved them. Expressing your feelings, learning how to express your feelings.

It wasn't a bad idea, he supposed, once you got over the initial shock.

Maybe he'd try it.

Chapter 6

One thing about Patrick, he loved to go to parties but, once there, he clammed up and stowed himself in a corner and acted like a nerdy hermit.

He and Patrick had sworn off girls. Not that they'd ever sworn on. Neither of them seemed to have the knack for girls, Tim often thought. They were able to give each other the bends, telling tall tales they concocted, jokes that reduced them to quivering blobs. But all their imagination dried up in the presence of the opposite sex. Girls seemed to stampede from them in droves, probably afraid of being corralled and bored to death.

If he'd had a sister, things might have been different. As a girl, she would have known about other girls, and could have clued him in on all sorts of magical approaches. Patrick had a sister. Her name was Melissa. She was thirteen and ugly. Patrick said there was nothing in this world uglier than a thirteen-year-old sister.

"Sure there are, plenty of things," he said.

"Name some."

He tried to and failed.

Melissa weighed more than Patrick did. She played tennis and basketball and field hockey, all to win. Melissa took tap-dancing lessons. She had special tap-dancing shoes, whose soles were overlaid with heavy metal at the toes. You could hear Melissa tap dancing all over town, Patrick said.

Patrick also said Tim shouldn't feel bad about not having a sister.

"What they do is," Patrick said, "they use up all the hot water. Plus, they're always having slumber parties. Once I told my mother I wanted to have a slumber party, and she acted like I was a pervert."

Patrick said he had to shave three times a week—except his cheeks were as rosy and smooth as a baby's behind, no matter what he said. Everyone in Patrick's family had red hair. Patrick's father had only a little rim of red hair trailing around behind his ears. Patrick was resigned to being bald, eventually, he said, if he lived long enough.

This summer, Tim and Patrick planned on hiking

the Appalachian Trail. They would start at Mount Katahdin in Maine and keep going until they hit Georgia. He hadn't told his mother yet. She'd only start worrying about a bear grabbing him out of his sleeping bag and swallowing him whole. Or, in her mind's eye, she'd see a knife-wielding weirdo hanging out in the men's room, ready to spring on the first sixteen-year-old innocent who came in to take a leak.

"You want to hear about the hundred and fifty Spanish dudes in the Pyrenees who wanted wives?" Patrick asked. "I read it in the paper." Tim didn't bother to answer, knowing there was no way in the world he could stop Patrick from telling him about the hundred and fifty Spanish dudes in the Pyrenees who wanted wives. Once on course, Patrick was rarely, if ever, deflected.

"They're all lonely bachelors, see, so they decide they'll advertise in the paper for wives, the way they did in the olden days. They put in this ad saying they're looking for a hundred and fifty women to marry. Next thing you know, the Pyrenees are swarming with a hundred and fifty dames rattling around, looking for the lonely dudes who're looking for wives.

"Then, you know what happened? Those dudes keep hanging out in the local bar and grill, as always, tossing horseshoes, leaning on the pinball machine, all like that, chewing the fat. Paying the dames no mind at all. Next thing, the girls get disgusted and take off to where they came from, without so much as getting pinched, even. And the dudes are left high and dry and as lonely as ever." Patrick shook his head sadly. "That's us, Tim," he said. "Lonely bachelors who don't know squat about what makes the fair sex tick."

"Hey, speak for yourself," he told Patrick. "I'm into writing love letters." Until he'd said it, he hadn't actually decided.

"The price of stamps just went up, and you decide to start writing love letters." Patrick rolled his eyes. "Your timing stinks."

"I said I was into writing them, not necessarily mailing them." It was definitely helpful to talk things out, to put stuff into words to get a clearer picture of what you were thinking about in the first place. He felt as if he'd taken a giant step in the right direction.

"If you're going to write those letters, you have to send them to somebody. Else you'll be just like those Spanish dudes—all talk and no action," Patrick said.

"That's my middle name," he said.

"And there's always the possibility of breach of promise," Patrick told him. "That's when she sues you because you promised to marry her in writing and then you backed out."

"So who's talking marry? I only want to be pals.

49

Honest, Patrick, you should read some of those old love letters. Those guys were full of it. A lot of sensuous desire was going on back then. A lot of heavy breathing. Hearts and souls and Death with a capital D. Carriages pulling out at dawn."

"Hey, hey." Patrick looked interested. "Do they cover whips and studded wristbands and black leather?"

"You can't have everything," he said. "But some of the stuff they put down on paper is so outrageous you wouldn't believe it. I wouldn't dare write some of the things they write. So I invent."

"You could always copy," Patrick said.

"Copy?" The idea had been noodling around in his head. Copy. "But somebody might sue me for plagiarism. If you copy something word for word, that's plagiarism, isn't it?"

"We're talking love letters here, son, not stuff for publication. All those cats that wrote the letters are daid, right? You're not planning on publishing their letters for money, passing them off as yours, are you? So what's your prob?" Patrick's shoulders brushed the tips of his ears, and his palms turned upward as he made his point.

"I read in the paper about a kid who entered a short story contest," Tim said. "He copied a story O. Henry or somebody famous wrote, copied it down word for word. Then he signed his name and entered it in the contest."

"What happened?"

"He won first prize. The judges liked his work. They thought he showed talent. Thought he should be encouraged to make writing his life's work."

"Smart judges," Patrick said. "What was the prize? A trip for two to Australia?" Ever since he was little, Patrick had wanted to go to Australia to try for a ride in a kangaroo's pouch.

"I don't know. But, to follow through, some guy pointed out the story had been written by O. Henry, or whoever it was, and the judges found the story in a collection of famous short stories. Then they called in the kid's father and the kid admitted he'd lifted it verbatim from the book. 'OK, so I stole it,' the kid said. 'So what?'"

He and Patrick shook their heads. "Dumb," Patrick said. "Really dumb. And arrogant. How arrogant can you get?"

"They can't send him to jail for trying, can they? I mean, no money was involved." Tim had checked the paper for a week after, looking for some follow-up, but there'd been nothing.

"They might give him ten years for trying," said Patrick. "Either that or take up ditch digging instead."

"Patrick?"

"I'm listening."

"What do you think your soul looks like? If you could see it, I mean, what would it remind you of?"

Patrick considered. "A hard-boiled egg."

Trust Patrick.

"How about yours?" Patrick wanted to know.

"I think mine might look like a laser beam."

"Try telling Sister Mary Teresa that." Sister Mary Teresa was the nun who had instructed them both in catechism before they'd made their first communion. In addition to having them commit the Ten Commandments to memory, as well as the Hail Mary and the Lord's Prayer, Sister Mary Teresa had kept them in line by intimidation and sheer strength of will. Sister Mary Teresa was small but fierce, Tim recalled. One look from those little dark eyes and you knew you'd done something requiring penance, even if you couldn't think of what it was. Three decades of the rosary might fix things up, if you were lucky.

Patrick said he had it on good authority that Sister Mary Teresa was a midget. A tall midget, Patrick said. No matter. When Sister Mary Teresa laid one of her tiny hands on you, for whatever reason, there went the ball game, so to speak.

Still, they tried.

The memory of Danny Brennan running off at the mouth about Sister Mary Teresa, when Danny hadn't known she was around, was still fresh in their minds, even though it had happened long ago. Danny had just gotten warmed up, telling about Sister Mary Teresa being arrested for shoplifting, not knowing she was approaching from the rear on her little cat feet. The expression on Danny's face when he saw her was memorable. She propelled him before her like a hostage, and when he emerged from her office, Danny Brennan was a beaten man. You didn't fool around with Sister Mary Teresa, if you were smart.

"Yeah, actually, I was thinking of engaging Sister Mary Teresa in a philosophical discussion about souls and stuff," he told Patrick. "I have to get my act together first, though."

"I'd hate to have to hang around until you get your act together," Patrick said.

Chapter 7

"Hey, Sophie, how's tricks?"

He couldn't believe he'd said it. Last night he'd tossed and turned, trying to get what was to be his spontaneous witticism just right. It seemed to have lost something in the translation.

Sophie looked startled and ducked her head so her chin was almost resting on her chest.

"Remember me?" He'd sworn he wouldn't say that. "I was mowing the grass next door when you sat on Benjy. I let you out of the bathroom. Remember?"

He'd blown it. No two ways about it, he'd blown it but good.

"Oh," said Sophie, remembering. "Yeah. Sorry I got mad. I was pretty uptight. I can't stand to be locked in anyplace."

She raised her head and looked straight at him. Her eyes were gray! And all along he'd thought they were blue. Amazing! Absolutely amazing.

"My brother locked me in the closet when I was really little, and I can still remember the feeling of panic. I always panic when I'm locked in. I'm claustrophobic, you see."

"How do you do on an airplane?" he asked, impressed by her easy use of "claustrophobic."

"I've never been on one. And maybe I never will. I fight it, but it's no good. I'm not afraid of anything else," she said defensively. "Just that one thing."

"That's OK. I'm afraid of snakes and porcupines."

"You are?" He could see he'd hit a nerve. Already she liked him better. God, if he'd known that would do it, he could've thrown in a few more things he was afraid of. Roller coasters. Girls. His little voice told him, "Quit while you're ahead." Maybe she'd like him now that she knew he wasn't Attila the Hun. Nothing like sharing a few phobias to cement a friendship.

Sophie wore a red-and-black plaid shirt made of some hairy fabric. He longed to reach out and touch her, to get the feel of it—the fabric, not her. But he was too smart for that. He knew better than to touch her. This girl would take a lot of getting to know before he knew her. If he ever did.

"Hi, Soph." A girl wearing a sweater about eight

55

sizes too big for her stood there, looking at them, her eyes curious. "What's up?"

"Nothing much," said Sophie. The girl tapped her foot and twirled a piece of her hair around and around, never letting her gaze drop. "This is my friend Barbara," Sophie said. He nodded at Barbara, who nodded back. "This is Tim." Sophie concluded her introductions, addressing the words to the air over Barbara's head. His heart soared. She knew his name!

Later, eating lunch in the cafeteria, he told Patrick, "I think I might have a crush on her."

"It's all those letters you been reading." Patrick checked out a banana for black spots, which freaked him out. "They'd give an aardvark ideas. Shooting you full of sensuous desire. Man. What you do now is, you ask her out." Patrick popped part of the banana in his mouth and discarded the rest. "That's what you do when you have a crush on a girl. You ask her out."

"Where do we go? And how do we get there?" Tim wanted to know. "I don't have my license yet, and even after I get it, I'll bet my mother will still be there in the passenger seat, wringing her hands and jamming on the brakes every time we come to a red light. She's always afraid I won't see it and I'll go right through and cause a five-car pileup. Probably she'll be in the passenger seat on my first date, too, keeping her eye on me. My date will be stashed in the back," he ended mournfully.

"Entirely possible," Patrick agreed, making him feel worse. "Mothers are everywhere. Ask Sophie to the basketball game. Tell her you'll meet her inside. That way you won't have to pick her up or take her home. Or buy her a corsage."

"A corsage!" he almost shouted. "Who wears a corsage to a basketball game? You are some weird dude, Patrick, you know that?"

Undisturbed, Patrick said, "All you have to do is sit next to her and you both watch the game. You don't have to talk to her or anything. That way, if you don't like her, or she doesn't like you, you're not out any bucks. If you meet her inside, she has to pay for herself, right? OK, so right away, you're ahead of the game." Patrick snapped his fingers, pleased with himself. "Then, after, if you guys really interface and all, you ask her if she's thirsty. She says yes, so you buy her a Coke."

"Patrick, you are so full of it."

"In my other life," said Patrick smugly, "I had plenty of dates. I was a regular Don Juan with the girls." Patrick was into reincarnation. In his life before this one, he said, he'd been a *doge* in a palazzo in Venice. "You shoulda seen me in a gondola," Patrick bragged. "Singing 'O Sole Mio,' sailing up and down the Grand Canal, and fighting off the crowds of señoritas crawling all over me."

"There aren't any señoritas in Italy, Patrick," he

57

said. "You're sure it was the Grand Canal? Sounds to me like you're confused."

Patrick grinned. "Hey, it was me who was there, not you, Tim. You had to be there. Seeing is believing, right?"

Patrick could make you believe anything. Almost anything.

"Whatever you do," Patrick got back to the matter at hand, "don't go steady. If you go steady, then you have to start going to her house for Sunday dinner, start sending her corsages, making nice with her old man, remembering her birthday. Stuff like that. It gets really involved."

"I haven't even asked her to a basketball game yet," he said. "You're moving too fast for me."

"The thing about love letters, you have to ask for 'em back after you break up," Patrick sailed on without a pause. "I read that somewhere in one of those girls' mags that Melissa gets. You'd be amazed what you can pick up from them. Otherwise, if she doesn't give 'em back, the love letters, I mean, she might show 'em to her friends, and they'd have a field day, laughing up a storm at all the dumb things you wrote, and word would get out that you're some super cluck and, boy, would they make fun of you! You don't want that to happen, do you? The best thing, Tim, is not to write her love letters, just call her on the phone and talk lovey-dovey all you want. That way, unless her old man's running a tap on the phone, it's only your word against hers."

"What if I write love letters to her and she won't give 'em back when we break up? And how can we break up when we've never had a date?"

Patrick shook his head. "If she refuses to return your letters, she's not worthy of you in the first place, Tim."

"Man," he grumbled, "this has to be the shortest courtship on record! One minute I'm telling her to meet me inside the gym to see the basketball game, the next she won't give me back my love letters. What do I do now?"

"You're on the fast track, son," Patrick told him, patting him on the back. "But you got yourself into this mess, you get yourself out."

Chapter 8

Saturday morning his father called to say he and Joy were going to the driving range to hit some golf balls, did he want to come along?

"Sure," he said, not really wanting to go. "Sure, that'd be great, Dad." If it'd been just him and his father, fine, but Joy made him self-conscious.

His mother had gone to an auction with Kev. He wrote a note telling her where he'd gone. "A thousand greetings from yr. loving son," he signed it. Seeing as how he was her only son, there'd be no confusion there.

Silently he stalked through the house, imagining himself a pirate out for the plunder. The stereo was old and not worth carrying. The camera was an unreliable Polaroid. The silver was plate and also heavy. His mother had no furs or jewels. About the only thing worth stealing was his bike, a sixteenth-birthday present from both his parents. They had chipped in to buy it for him, which fact touched him greatly. A touring bike, complete with aerodynamic saddle, easy highroll pressure tires, and a fully lugged hand-built frame; it was so beautiful, he was almost afraid to ride it, for fear it might get banged up. That bike was the Rolls Royce of bikes. He kept it polished to a high gloss, and he had had the best lock made to lock it up anytime he took it out. If he had his way, he'd also install an alarm system on it, rigged to blast off at the police station if someone so much as laid a pinky on it.

His father said they'd be around for him at about ten. He had almost an hour to kill. He scrubbed out the shower stall, his weekly chore, and swabbed down the kitchen floor for good measure. The kitchen was, by his lights, the nicest room in the house. He had helped his mother hang the wallpaper, which was bright and cheerful, and together, they'd done a good job.

Chores over, he hit the book. As he took the stairs two at a time, he thought, somewhat sheepishly, that the world's best love letters had become an obsession with him. Whenever he settled down with them for a good read, he was swept away on a tide of feeling that no other book he'd ever read had produced. He felt almost as if he'd written those letters himself.

One he liked in particular. He had its place marked

61

in the book so he could turn directly to it without wasting a moment. Now he read it aloud to an empty room.

"I am at your tiny feet, beloved—I kiss them, I roll myself under the soles of them and place them on the nape of my neck—I sweep my hair with the places where you are to walk and prostrate myself under your footprints."

Crazy. A foot nut. A foot fetishist.

The writer of the letter was Franz Liszt, composer, pianist, born 1811, died 1886. Franz Liszt, lover boy, writer of Liszt's *Hungarian Rhapsody*. A pianist of note at age nine. A true weirdo.

Outside, his father honked, summoning him to the golf range. He shoved the book under his pillow, where it would be waiting when he returned from his triumphal golf debut.

He hopped into the backseat. Joy turned to look at him. "Oh, Tim," she said, wrinkling her nose. He'd noticed she wrinkled her nose a lot. Apparently it was the barometer of her emotions. Right now she was registering dismay.

"You're not going like that, are you?" Joy said softly.

"I'm clean," he said, looking down at himself.

"Like what?" his father said.

"We're not going anyplace fancy, are we?" Tim asked. "I thought we were just going to hit some balls at the driving range." He smiled out the window, wishing he'd never come. "I mean, we're not going to a club or anything, are we?"

People worry too much about what they put on their backs, he thought. One suit of clothes for funerals and weddings and one pair of what he'd called "party shoes" when he was little ought to take care of everything. He liked clothes that were effortless. Soft, old clothes. One of his favorite sayings was "Dress comfortably." He thought Joy was a trifle over-dressed, to tell the truth. But he wouldn't have thought to comment on her clothes. She had no right to comment on his.

This promises to be a fun-filled morning, he thought.

"Keep your head down and your elbows in, Tim. And keep your eye on the ball." Old Joy, it turned out, was a golf instructor, as well as a computer programmer. She sounded like the guys on TV who give thirty-second-spot golf lessons between rounds of a tournament.

"You have a nice swing, Tim, but you simply have to keep your eye on the ball." This after he'd taken several swings at the ball and missed it completely. Whiffs, they were called. Talk about humiliation. Try swinging at an inanimate object and missing it. He had heard that golf could be a humiliating game.

Next to them a kid of about ten was getting golf lessons from his father. The father had a short fuse, and every time the kid swung at the ball the father brought out a little booklet and read the dos and don'ts of the game to the kid in a loud voice. The kid was nearly in tears. Fun thing to do on a Saturday morning. Beats playing softball.

Tim and his father drove golf balls under Joy's watchful, narrowed eyes. Instructions flowed from between her thin, tight lips. Maybe his father's next girlfriend, or neighbor, whatever, would turn out to be something simple, like a snorkeler. He certainly hoped so. His watch, a Swatch watch, was guaranteed to be good as far as a hundred feet underwater. He'd always wanted to test it out.

"How about if we play a couple of holes instead of just hitting the balls?" There was a nine-hole course adjacent to the driving range. "I figure that way I might get the idea quicker."

With a swift, graceful motion, Joy set up a tee, put a ball on it, stood up, swung, and sent the ball soaring.

"Beautiful," his father said. "Beautiful." And his father looked at him, encouraging him to encourage Joy. He said it was beautiful, too.

"You don't want to bother with that pitch-and-putt course, Tim," Joy told him, her voice leaving no room for argument. "After you get the hang of it, I'll take you to my club for a game."

Not me, he vowed silently. You're not getting me on your club course. Obediently, he and his father drove balls until the bucket was empty.

A heavyset man with a ruddy face came out of the office.

"Morning, folks," he greeted them. "Enjoying yourselves?"

"Fine, thanks," his father said. Joy turned her back on the man and put on her golf sweater, yellow to match the rest of her outfit. A chill wind had come up. Dark clouds swarmed.

"Len Feeley," the large-nosed man said, extending a hand. His father and Len Feeley shook hands. Feeley was Sophie's last name.

Mr. Feeley (he began an imaginary dialogue). I'm seriously thinking of having a crush on your daughter. In fact, I may have one already. I may ask her to a basketball game. OK with you?

"You don't find what you want, let me know. We aim to please." And Len Feeley lifted his lips in what was surely a smile.

It began to rain.

"Come inside, if you want, till it stops," Len said. The kid next to them took off. "It's only a shower, Eddie! Come back!" the father yelled. The kid kept on going.

When his father dropped him off at the house, Joy said, "We'll do it again real soon, Tim."

"Sure you won't have a sandwich with us, Tim?" his father asked.

"Thanks, Dad, but I have work to do, letters to write." His father's face expressed astonishment. "Since when have you become a letter writer?" his father asked.

"I'm trying it on for size," he said. "Expanding my horizons. Thanks for the golf, Dad."

"Don't be discouraged, Tim!" Joy cried. He waved, and watched until the car rounded the corner before he went inside.

Chapter 9

If Sophie had ever made goo-goo eyes at him, made
any kind of flirtatious move, he might've lost interest.
As it was, her aloofness, her don't-touch-me air fanned
the fires of love burning in his insides. Sophie was
her own person. No one was getting within easy distance of Sophie until she gave the go-ahead signal.
Theirs would be an old-fashioned romance, he decided. He would woo her with sweet words, bunches
of daisies plucked from the fields, and an occasional
Milky Way bar to let her know how sweet he thought
she was. They would have long, heartfelt discussions
about everything in the world worth discussing. He
would tell her his innermost thoughts, as she would
tell him hers. He would tell her how he felt about
her, would put his deepest feelings into words, so she

would know exactly how deep his love was. Sophie, he knew, was the kind of girl who would give back his love letters without even being asked. If and when they broke up, which they might or might not do.

Maybe he could hang the blame for copying the love letter on Patrick. Hadn't the conversation about the bozo who'd copied an O. Henry short story and entered it in a contest sparked the whole thing? He couldn't be sure. Maybe it was his inability to conjure up enough flowery words on his own that made him decide to copy one of the *One Hundred of the World's Best Love Letters* and mail it to his beloved Sophie. Anonymously. It would have to be anonymously. If he signed his name, he would be a plagiarist, no matter what Patrick said, and romance would probably fly out the window, and they'd wind up hating each other. Well, she'd hate him. He could never hate her.

He wanted to send her a proper love letter, not one written by a randy, sixteen-year-old undercover intellectual. Sophie deserved only the best. Sophie deserved a love letter straight from the pen of one of the world's masters.

Time and again, in his search for the ultimate in love letters, he returned to Franz Liszt—composer, pianist, foot fetishist.

"If you knew how languorously and furiously I have need of you!" old Franz wrote to the Countess

D'Agoult, year unknown. "I can do nothing but dream of you! I cannot talk to anyone and to you even less than the others!" See, even old Franz had difficulty talking to the girl of his heart, which undoubtedly was why he resorted to writing torrid love letters, and why he couldn't seem to breathe without his exclamation point.

"If you knew only half the happiness it would be to me to see you here tomorrow, the day after tomorrow, I would not hesitate to say to you, 'Come Marie, Marie. . . .' "

Come, Sophie, Sophie. Substitute Sophie and it read much better.

"Let your beautiful head bend voluptuously again to mine, let your adorable tears . . ."

Could a head bend voluptuously? He stood in front of the mirror bending his head this way and that, shooting tender glances at himself. The mirror's reflection sent him back a twit looking in need of some milk of magnesia. Maybe females were able to bend their heads voluptuously. It was beyond him.

Scratch "adorable tears." Mind bending. No such thing existed. He didn't want to alienate Sophie, freak her out. He only wanted to make an indelible impression to pave the way for something big.

Maybe it would be wise to combine the best parts of the Liszt letters, working in the bit about the tiny feet. It also occurred to him that Sophie might not want him, or anyone else, for that matter, to kiss her feet. He sure wouldn't want her kissing his.

"Oh, how I long to see you again, dear masterpiece of God." Old Franz was really warming up now. Also getting heavy. "Dear masterpiece of God" sounded slightly ridiculous, also slightly sacrilegious to him. Not to mention going too far. Scratch it.

"How could I help adoring the Good God who created you, so good, so beautiful, so perfect, so made to be cherished, adored and loved to death and madness."

There were no two ways about it; death and madness caught the eye, made one pause and think. His handwriting sprawled ungracefully across the paper, lending a certain *je ne sais quoi* to the words. On the other hand, if Sophie was one for taking sentences apart, dissecting each and every word, she might conceivably take exception to being loved to death and madness. It was hard, deciding what to leave in, what to take out. He was in the position of censoring Franz Liszt. Not too many people he knew could make that statement. Writing a love letter was not an easy job, he decided. Even if it wasn't an original love letter.

The phone rang.

"Hello, fool," Patrick said.

"Can't talk now. I'm working on something really

big." If he quit now, before he finished, he might chicken out and not finish at all. He had to get his letter in the mail before he lost his nerve.

"You want to play some pool?" Patrick's father had given the family a pool table for Christmas. Patrick's mother had been outraged at first, said she didn't want her children picking up bad habits. Now Patrick's mother was the star pool player in the family. Melissa was second.

"Later. I'll come over after I'm done."

The words plunged across paper, faster than he could get them down. Slow down, he warned himself. Slow down. Or she won't be able to read a word. His handwriting, he realized, had taken on the look of ancient hieroglyphics as urgency and artistry drove him forward, ever forward. He had never felt as close to anyone as he felt right now to Sophie. This was for her. He hardly knew her, yet writing these words of love, Franz Liszt's words of love, overblown, high-falutin, made his and Sophie's romance seem real. What a terrific thing he was doing! Copying from the masters. Sophie would be overwhelmed; maybe she'd be his forever.

But how would she know who had sent her the letter? He couldn't sign his name. And, if he didn't sign his name, he wouldn't get credit for it. It was a dilemma. He would have to be Anon. Sophie would have to fall in love with Anonymous, old silver-tongued Anon.

There was more. "The day will come when we shall see and comprehend clearly what at present we can only dimly glimpse and hope for in our terrestrial darkness . . . then you will recall the burning words that neither you nor I could have held back, for they would have shattered our bones."

Way to go, Franz. What a wrap-up. Lay it all out. Shattered bones and all. He thought of adding a row of kisses, XXXXX, as a final expression of the high esteem in which he held Sophie, and decided that, in view of what had gone before, the XXXXX would be an anticlimax.

Sighing, he jotted down, on a separate piece of paper, various possible ways he might sign his letter. "God bless thee!" was one. "In haste, I am forever yours," another. "Your patient and humble servant" didn't grab him.

"Yours, Anon." That would do it, have to do it. Selecting one of his mother's envelopes, he donned a pair of her gloves before slipping the letter inside. Thereby eliminating all fingerprints. A theatrical move that pleased him greatly. All that remained was to find a stamp.

"Hey, Ma, got a stamp?"

"Look at this, Tim." She was poring over an

arrangement of old coins she had spread out on the tabletop. She held up a coin blackened with years and they both studied it with attention.

"Isn't this handsome?" His mother turned the coin in her hand.

"Cool, Ma, but can I borrow a stamp from you?"

"What on earth for?"

"To mail a letter, what else?" said he, pretending that he mailed letters frequently. Don't give me heat now, Ma, he begged her silently. I might cave in and tear it up. Please, Ma, no heat.

She looked at him in a puzzled way, which he ignored.

"In the righthand desk drawer, Tim," she said. "Help yourself."

"Thanks, Ma!" he shouted in sudden elation. "You're some sweet masterpiece of God, all right!"

He slammed out of the house, whistling, leaving her with her mouth open, astonished.

When he reached the mailbox, he had second thoughts. To mail, or not to mail. Faint heart never won nothing. A favorite pithy saying he'd dreamed up. On the other hand, it seemed a dubious thing to do, now that he was here, letter in hand, Sophie's name and address culled from the phone book, writ in large letters, zip code and all.

Sometimes, he reflected later, life's biggest decisions are based on small, inconsequential events. As he stood there, it seemed to him the letter moved in his hand. His soul was inside that letter. The mail truck pulled up, the driver got out, unlocked the box, and loaded its contents into a Postal Service bag. The mailman looked at him. "You want me to take that?" he said. "I'm running late as it is."

Tim looked down at the letter. "I'm not sure I have the right address on it," he said.

"Always put your return address on the back. That way you get it back, if it's not right," the mailman said.

"I don't want her to know who sent it," he blurted out.

The mailman's eyebrows went out of control. "Oh, one of those, huh? You got to watch what you send through the U.S. mails, buddy. They got all kinds of laws. You can get sent away two, maybe even three years, if you don't watch your step. You look like a nice kid. I wouldn't want to see you in trouble. But you want to be careful what you send through the mail. We got very strict rules."

Maybe the mailman thought it was a bomb, albeit a skinny, tiny one. And that he was an anarchist.

"Also, too," the mailman continued, "you want to watch what you put down on paper. Once or twice, I myself let the heart rule the old noggin. Resulting in nothing but sad news, I'm sorry to say. But you live, you learn. It's your life, buddy. I'm running late, like I said. Make up your mind." The mailman tossed the bulging bag into his truck.

"Take it," he said, thrusting the letter into the man's hand. "It's now or never."

"Way to go," the mailman said, hopping back into the truck. "Hope you stay out of jail!" he hollered before he drove away.

"You and me both, buddy," Tim said.

Chapter 10

When Melissa answered his knock and saw him standing there, her hand flew to cover a cluster of zits that had settled on her chin. In a slightly muffled voice she said, "I didn't know you were coming over."

He smiled at her.

"Come on in. Patrick's downstairs, practicing," Melissa said. "I beat him five games last night, playing pool. He's sore. Patrick's a sore loser, know that? My mother and I can take him on and my father any day, and wipe up the floor with them."

Melissa's hair was done up in fat pink curlers. Without her glasses, her eyes were pale, luminous, myopic. He noticed the zipper on her jeans didn't quite close, leaving a small portion of Melissa hanging out. He averted his eyes, thinking of what Patrick had said about a thirteen-year-old sister being the ugliest thing in the world. Melissa would improve, he figured. She had nowhere to go but up. Her nose was a little lop-sided and the zits didn't help. And she could definitely stand to drop ten, maybe fifteen, pounds. Outside of that, Melissa was all right.

"What grade you in these days, Melissa?" he asked, being friendly.

"Eighth," she answered, hand still over her chin. She wore a gray sweatshirt that declared "I Wanna Rock."

"Tim," she said hesitantly, "don't tell Patrick I asked you, but I want to ask you something. Privately."

Melissa cast a cold eye over her shoulder, ready to nail Patrick if he showed himself.

"Ask away," he said, feeling very mature, flattered that she wanted to consult with him, ask his advice.

"Well, we're having this dance. That is, at my school. It's sort of a fund-raising dance combined with a grad-uation party. Graduation from eighth grade?"

Melissa was asking him, not telling him, and he began to feel uneasy. Was she going to hit him up for money, he wondered, slapping noisily at his empty pockets. "Yeah? Go on, Melissa."

Melissa took down her hand and the zits seemed to leap out at him.

"I'm broke, Melissa," he said. "Sorry, I can't help."

"It's not that." Her face was very earnest and her cheeks were stained a deep red.

He waited, listening, hoping for sounds of Patrick approaching.

"We're supposed to ask a boy, see," Melissa said in a rush. "I was hoping you'd be my date."

He was stunned. Absolutely knocked on his ear. Go to a dance with Patrick's thirteen-year-old sister, who was in the eighth grade? Melissa went to St. Raymond's parochial school, the very same school in which he and Patrick had received their religious instructions before they made their first communion.

As if she read his mind, Melissa said, "I'm almost fourteen. That is—I'll be fourteen in six weeks, or so."

"Uh," he said, as if someone had hit him in the stomach. They stood there, looking at each other. "I don't know how to dance, Melissa." Which was the plain truth. "I never went to dancing school."

"That's all right." She seemed to feel better now that she'd spoken her piece. She waved her arms around and her feet moved as if to silent music, though she wore no headset, no earphones. "I can't really, either. Nobody dances at these dances, anyway. They just sort of stand around and pig out."

Once, twice, he tried to find the right words to turn her down. He even resorted to a choking fit, fighting desperately for time.

Gasping, eyes tearing up, he finally said, "How come you don't ask one of the boys in your class?" blinking at her as if a bright light had been turned on suddenly, blinding him.

Melissa put her hands on her hips. "Because," she said, "they're all smaller than me. Than I. I'm the biggest girl in the class." Suddenly, without warning, Melissa's face turned downward completely, like a sad clown's. Mouth, eyes, eyebrows, even her nose seemed to dip down as she spoke. A terrible silence fell, broken only by the sound of him swallowing. All the saliva seemed to have left his mouth.

"It's only a tea dance!" Melissa wailed, tossing her head, sending the pink curlers on a wild wobble.

"A tea dance?" He had never heard of such a thing. This was even worse than he'd thought. "A tea dance," he repeated, trying to stay calm.

"Yeah. From four to six. On Sunday. Please, Tim." Melissa's huge eyes glistened at him. "Will you please, Tim? If you won't go with me, I won't go either. You're my only hope."

"Can't you find someone else to take you?" he asked, almost pleading with her. "I think I'm busy Sunday. I don't think I can go, Melissa."

For Pete's sake, kid, I just spent hours composing a steamy love letter to this girl. A tea dance. Kid stuff. A pig-out tea dance, for God's sake. Go play with your pals, Melissa, and leave me alone.

Melissa stood close to him, smelling of shampoo and onions.

"You wouldn't even have to dance with me, Tim," she said. "All they do anyway is stand around, the girls, I mean, and the boys do the same thing. They tell jokes and burp and, you know, laugh. We wouldn't have to stay the whole time. We could just stay a little while. Just so they'd see you were my date." By now, she was so close her breath tickled his ear.

"And I'd pay, Tim. It wouldn't cost you a nickel. I promise. My mother's buying the tickets, anyway. Please, Tim?"

He couldn't look at her.

"Why don't you get Patrick to take you?" he whispered, ashamed.

Melissa jumped as if stung by a wasp, a whole nest of wasps. "I'd die first!" she shouted. The color left her face and he was afraid she might be having an attack of something, might even faint. "I'd absolutely die rather than go with my own brother!"

At the word "brother" Melissa let out a low gurgling sound, like an unplugged drain.

"Hey Tim!" Patrick popped into view. "I didn't know you were here. What're you doing, chewing the fat with Fatty? Let's go down and shoot some pool."

Melissa turned and ran. He stumbled after Patrick, falling upon the pool table as if it was an oasis and he a traveler tuckered out after crossing the Sahara. Patrick tossed him a cue and a piece of chalk, to take the slipperiness off the tip of the cue, Patrick said, as if he'd been playing pool since he was a pup.

Patrick beat him one game; then, by a fluke, he beat Patrick. The cool joy of winning was heady and unfamiliar to him. He was not a winner at sports, or at much of anything. There was nothing like coming in first, he decided, hoping to make a habit of it. Patrick's father showed up and beat both of them. Fortunately, for one and all, Patrick's mother and Melissa were otherwise occupied.

Buoyed by winning a game, Patrick's father was all set to make an afternoon of it. But, "I have to get going," Tim said, still thinking about the tea dance and wondering if he could dredge up somebody to escort her. He liked Melissa, felt sorry for her. It was tough to be thirteen, a girl, and ugly. He felt sorry for her, but not sorry enough to say he'd go to the dance with her.

On his way out, through the kitchen, he ran into Patrick's mother, who was stirring a huge vat of chili. He liked her and she liked him, too. Patrick had told him that. "She says you have a kind heart," Patrick had said, and he had been terribly pleased. Melissa stood at the sink, back to him, as he stopped to talk briefly to Patrick's mother. Melissa's mother, too, if

81

you wanted to be persnickety. Because he felt guilty about turning Melissa down, he was extra talkative and polite to her mother. Guilt does funny things to people. When Melissa turned to say something to her mother, he saw her face. She was puffed up like a blowfish, probably from crying. He felt like a rat.

If only St. Raymond's would throw a beer bash for the eighth-grade graduation, he might reconsider. But he was darned if he'd be caught in a tea-dance trap. The telephone rang and Melissa's mother answered. "It's for you, Missy."

Melissa spoke in a low voice, but he heard her say, "No, he won't. No, I won't. I don't care. I'm not going by myself and that's that."

He opened the kitchen door and a gust of wind entered, uninvited. A little voice in his head said "Get going or you'll be sorry." He knew that voice. Ninety-nine percent of the time it was right.

"About that dance," he heard himself say. Melissa turned and gave him a terrible look, full of hope. He was aware of her mother standing by the sink, spoon held high, frozen, as if someone was taking her picture.

"I guess I can handle it," he said. It was as if another person was talking, saying things he himself would never have said. "It's OK, Melissa. I'll go."

He knew he would never, ever, forget her expression.

"Oh, Tim." She clasped her hands and a blinding light lit her face. Followed by a smile of such unmitigated happiness he was embarrassed.

He thought he heard Patrick coming. He had to get out of there before Patrick showed his face.

"I'll be seeing you," he said. For now, the important thing was to keep going, to make space between himself and Melissa, his tea-dance date.

"You'll be sorry," his little voice repeated. "Boy, will you ever be sorry!"

Chapter 11

One minute he'd been leading a practically monastic life, one totally devoid of women; the next, he had two bugging him. One he might want to get closer to, the other not.

Mournfully, he contemplated his situation, shaking his head the while, trying to stop the ringing inside it. Get your head on straight, buddy. His *beau geste*, for that was the way he saw his fine gesture made by telling Melissa he'd go to the dance, had put him in the pits. Bloody pig-out tea dance. He didn't even like tea. What an ass. Almost as bad as Kev, in a different way.

"You're my only hope," Melissa had said, and his sense of romance, of chivalry had been touched. Chivalry was dead but he'd dragged it, kicking and screaming, out of the grave. It didn't matter what had made him say he'd go. He'd said it. He was in a trap of his own making, the worst kind. He'd painted himself into a corner.

If it had been winter, he could've arranged a broken leg while skiing. A small price to pay, he figured. But it was almost summer, with dandelions rioting in the grass, and peonies about to pop.

Patrick, when he found out, would give him a hard time. Patrick would say he must've been playing without a full deck to say he'd go to a dance with Melissa. Patrick would shake his head and give him a lugubrious look. Patrick's lugubrious look was well honed and quite splendid.

If it'd been *his* sister, would Patrick have come to her rescue? Maybe. If someone had greased his palm with folding money. Patrick could be had for folding money. But he didn't have a sister.

A scene played itself against his eyelids every time he closed his eyes—him steering Melissa around St. Raymond's gym, keeping clear of the foul line. Clasping Melissa's substantial waist, sweating like a wrestler, trying to get a dialogue going with her. Avoiding collisions with the other dancers, eighth graders all, big-footed and pimply. He'd been an eighth grader once. He knew what eighth graders were like. Turkeys. Looking over Melissa's shoulder, trying to get a line on refreshments. How soon could he skin out? Half an hour? Fifteen minutes?

He groaned, imagining the tea dance. There was no out. He'd said he'd go and he had been taught to stick to his word.

Sophie should get the letter Monday. Or, if the mails fouled up, which they'd been known to do, Tuesday at the latest. On Wednesday, he would lie in wait. When he got her within his sights, he would study her face, check her for signs of mirth, sensuous desire, confusion. Rage? Anything was possible. Perhaps she'd fall into instant love with the writer of such purple prose. Or, perhaps, she would hate him. Would the strength of the written word bowl her over?

He lurked in corridors, skulked outside her homeroom, planning to accidentally bump into her as she exited the science lab. At last, he caught up with her, eating a bologna sandwich in the cafeteria. A dab of mustard marred her incomparable chin, and dozens of plastic bracelets marched jauntily up and down her arms as she chewed. He said, "Hi!" and registered amazement at finding her eating a bologna sandwich at lunch hour in the cafeteria. How strange that she should be here! Of all places! The palms of his hands were damp. Her friends giggled and poked her and one another. Sophie herself remained unmoved.

Expressionless. As he turned and walked away, he felt he'd lost that round. She thinks I'm a weirdo, he thought. And she's right.

That night, he began a second letter.

"Have your affections cooled?" he started out. "Since you have driven me from you, I am the least of mortals. I have lost all reason, all courage. You have taken everything from me! Sophie, my sweet Sophie, you will come again, will you not? Please accept this bouquet. When my hand presses my heart, you will know it is entirely occupied with you. To reply, you press your bouquet. Love me, my charming Sophie, and let not your hand ever leave your bouquet."

What if a bee got stuck in her bouquet and let Sophie have it? Was she even then supposed to hang on, sending love signals?

Like Patrick said, when you start getting crushes on a girl, next thing you know, you're sending corsages. And more. Much more.

He signed it "Yours, with sensuous desire, Anon.," trying to vary the ending of the first letter. On the other hand, that "sensuous desire" might, very probably would, give her the wrong idea. He crossed out "sensuous desire" and wound up with "Yours, Anon.," the same as before.

He placed the letter under his pillow. He would not send it right away. Tantalize her with his delay.

Besides, it needed a bit of editing here and there. Change a word here, a phrase there. He was striving for perfection. When it came to love letters, he was a perfectionist.

When he went downstairs, his mother was stretched out on the living-room couch. Not doing anything, just lying there, staring into space. That was unusual. She was seldom idle, preferring to knit or read, or, if her hands were empty and her face set into an intense expression, he knew she was adding figures in her head. It impressed him, the way she was able to do that. Once he'd offered her his calculator and she'd turned it down, saying she liked the mental exercise. A calculator, she said, was a crutch.

"Where's the trunk?" he asked at last, having searched high and low for it.

She turned her face to him and he saw it was blank. "What?"

"The old trunk, Ma. Where is it? I want to make sure I didn't leave any letters in it."

"Oh. Kev took it," she said. "He knows a man he thinks might be interested in buying it."

"When's he bringing it back?" He tried not to sound surly and knew, from his mother's face, that he hadn't succeeded.

"Tim, why do you always use that tone of voice when you mention Kev?" she asked. "What's he ever done to you?"

He shrugged. "Nothing. Sorry. I didn't know I had a special tone of voice for Kev."

"I want you two to like each other. I'm thinking of marrying Kev, Tim."

Before he could control himself, a loud, emphatic No! burst from him and lay there between them, separating them, sending out negative beeps. His mother sat up and smoothed her hair. She placed both feet primly together and stared down at them as if they had an answer to whatever the question was.

"Sorry," he said again. He felt his bones go loose, then tighten. He sat down in what used to be his father's chair.

"Sorry for what? Sorry I'm thinking of marrying Kev?"

"Sorry I said no," he answered. "If you want to marry Kev, that's your business."

"I know you don't like him. I wish you did. I know you think he's too young. Or that I'm too old, I'm not sure which." His mother smiled faintly.

"It's not only that."

"No? Then what is it, Tim?"

"Well, I guess you could say it's partly because I always hoped you and Dad might get back together." That was not a lie. That thought had crossed his mind several times with absolutely nothing to reinforce it. He had a friend whose divorced father had gotten married again. The kid said he hated his stepmother

at first, refused to call her anything but "Hey, you."
The kid admitted he'd behaved badly and now, after
two years, the kid said he really liked his stepmother.
And was sorry he'd behaved so wretchedly toward
her. But Tim had a feeling deep inside that, no matter
what, he'd never like Kev, that they would never be
friends. Kev was a phony, and if his mother didn't see
that, it wasn't up to him to tell her. They said that
love blinds people to the loved one's faults, and he
was willing to buy that. If he told his mother what he
thought of Kev and then she and Kev did get married,
he knew she'd never forget and maybe never forgive
him for what he'd said. So he kept his mouth shut.

"I would like for you to be happy, Ma," he told
her. "I would like for me to be happy, too. I always
remember Dad telling me that, when I was born, it
seemed life had treated him royally and that he'd never
been so happy. So I was dumb and naive, and thought
I was partly responsible for him being happy. I even
thought that as long as it was the three of us together,
we had it made. I know I was a jerk to think that.
But I was only a little kid. What did I know?"

His mother's face was frazzled and unhappy. She
rose from the couch and her movements were slow
and, it seemed to him, elderly. She had lost her former
girlishness, probably because of him.

"I'm tired, Tim," she said unnecessarily. "I'm going

90

to bed. If you want to go through the rest of the letters from the trunk, I put them in the lefthand desk drawer when you gave them back to me, along with the stamps. I knew you wanted them, so I didn't send them along with the trunk. Good night, Tim," she said, and he listened dolefully to the sound of her feet climbing the stairs.

Chapter 12

"Joy said to tell you she's sorry she can't make it for dinner tonight," his father said. "Her nephew's in town. She's taking him to see the sights."

"What sights? Which—Hojo's or McDonald's? There are no sights in this town." His mother slammed some pots and pans around noisily. She was in a bad mood, had been ever since the No! had popped out of him when she'd said she was thinking of marrying Kev. He and his mother, usually friends, were on the outs. He knew lots of kids who were perpetually on the outs with their mothers and, up to now, he'd had no sympathy for them.

"I didn't know Joy was supposed to be coming for dinner," his mother snapped, opening a can of tomatoes so violently tomato juice spewed over everything. "I'm a little tired of her coming here for dinner, especially when I didn't ask her, if you want to know the truth. She never brings even so much as a flower. Or a piece of candy."

His father mopped up the spilled juice and looked surprised. "I thought you hated to have people bring you candy because you eat it and get fat," he said.

His mother turned, slowly, majestically. "I am never fat," she said, pronouncing each word as if his father had just entered the country from Latvia and didn't understand a word of English.

"I thought you liked Joy," his father said in a wounded tone. "She likes you."

"Baloney. We hate each other and you know it. This is a very artificial situation, and I for one am calling it quits. If you want to come for dinner now and then, fine. But leave Joy home. Let her make her own dinner."

Time for him to get lost, he decided. Let them fight it out. It would be just like old times.

He retreated to his room to think. Sophie had given him no sign so far that she'd gotten the letter. But how could she when she didn't know he'd sent it? If anything, she paid less attention to him now than she had before, if such a thing was possible. He thought it entirely possible he could fall at Sophie's feet, foaming at the mouth and turning blue, and she'd step over

93

him as if he were invisible. He suspected her friend Barbara of bad-mouthing him, probably spreading nasty rumors about how he ate peas off his knife, about how he kicked little dogs, and about how he ate with his elbows on the table. Not to mention stealing little old ladies' Social Security checks the first of every month.

But he'd decided. Even if Sophie showed no sign that she'd received the first letter, tonight he was going to put the finishing touches on the second, which would be more passionate, more romantic than the first. His plan was to continue his barrage through the mails, each letter more fervent that the last, until Sophie was his.

It would be simpler, of course, to just pick up the telephone, dial Sophie's number, and when she answered, say, "How about it? Want to go steady?" Or, if that proved too abrupt, he could say, "How about a flick tonight?" Neither of these approaches grabbed him. The love letters were it.

Tonight, however, the words, his own or the real pros', seemed to have lost their charm. So he took down the old cigar box his father had given him. He had put the old letters from the trunk inside that box. When his father had presented it to him with a certain formality, saying, "I kept my stamp collection in this when I was your age, Tim. I want you to have it," he

94

had known his father, in his quiet way, was telling him how much he cared about his son.

"Thanks, Dad," he'd said. The box still smelled faintly of ancient cigars. Even the meager pile of letters smelled of old cigars. He rifled through the stack. Not all of them were letters of love. Several had been written in a spidery hand to someone named Mae, from her Aunt Nellie.

Well, weather here a little cooler as we had a good rain last night. It's been high eighties since Mon. Had some palpitations and went to Dr. to see what was what. Dr. said it was the heat, told me to lie with my feet up higher than my head when they started in. Jesse caught me with my feet in the air and thought I was passed out and having a fit. He threw a glass of water in my face to bring me around and ruined my new shirtwaist. Love, Aunt Nellie.

Every time he read that one, he laughed out loud. He could see Jesse throwing the glass of water in her face, see her jumping up and maybe chasing Jesse around the yard, waving a broom at him and hollering.

He put the cigar box back on his closet shelf and lay on his bed, fingers laced behind his head.

I don't want that turkey, Kev, for a stepfather, he thought. Why can't she find some bozo her own age, someone who loves her better than he loves himself, someone who doesn't carry an orange tent on his back like some sort of bizarre shell.

Turkey Kev sounded like a dish using leftover turkey in a new and delicious way, he thought. One that combined yogurt, tofu, and bean sprouts, perhaps. If his mother hadn't freaked out and lost her sense of humor, as she seemed to have done, he'd tell her that. And she'd come up with other ingredients to add to Turkey Kev. As it was, he kept his thoughts to himself.

A knock on the door made him spring to his feet. He didn't like anyone to find him lying down. They might think he was sick, or taking a nap. Neither of which he was.

"Oh, hi, Dad."

"Tim, just thought I'd ask if you'd like to go with Joy and me on Saturday to the driving range. Maybe you might like to give it another chance?" He noticed his father's sideburns had been trimmed down considerably.

"Sure, Dad, why not?" Why not indeed.

"Pick you up at ten, then," his father said.

"Great." His too-hearty voice rang insincerely in his own ears. He wondered how his father was going to break the news to Joy that she was persona non grata at the family dinner table. Maybe his mother was simply going through a hostile phase and would pass through it quickly and emerge on the other side. She loved to cook for people, loved having diners compliment her on the excellence of her cuisine. His mother could make three-day-old chicken taste like squab. Just ask her, she'd give you the recipe right off the top of her head. A pinch of thyme, a dash of basil, and it would melt in your mouth. Even its own mother wouldn't recognize it. She insisted on teaching him how to cook so that when he was on his own, she said, he wouldn't exist solely on hamburgers and scrambled eggs.

"Sophie, my angel," he said aloud. "My angel Sophie." Either one was bound to win her. Any girl would like being called my angel. Wouldn't she?

Chapter 13

Shortly after dawn on Saturday he rode his bike through the deserted streets of town, feeling like Robin Hood in search of the Appalachian Trail. With the wind at his back and the scent of the darling buds of May in his nose, he rode as if pursued by demons, straight into the rising sun. Only last week he'd seen *The Adventures of Robin Hood* on TV, starring the incomparable Errol Flynn. Now, there was a man. Fine legs and always a smile on his face. And what a swordsman. Even Basil Rathbone couldn't bring him to his knees.

A red pickup truck rattled by and the driver hailed him as if they were old friends. There was a definite feeling of camaraderie at being awake and on the move this early, he thought. He kept his eyes on the pavement, starred with cast-off pop tops, which always fooled him into thinking they were quarters. Last year alone he'd found, by eternal vigilance, three pennies and a dime.

Once town was behind him, he rode more slowly, patting the fenders of his bike now and then as he would have a horse's flanks—lovingly and with praise. It was a morning for poetry, and metaphors abounded. Clumps of complacent cows watched him pass. Frail, empty houses clung to the side of the road, their broken-down porches decorated with rickety rocking chairs nodding sleepily, as if ghosts sat there, taking a breather. Dogs came out at him as if he'd insulted their mothers—snarling, leaping, baring old teeth.

Not bad, he thought. A meadow massed with bright yellow and purple flowers caught his eye. He stopped, hoisted his bike over the stone wall that ringed the meadow, and dropped into the deep grass that lay on the other side. There he buried the bike in the tallest grass, a perfect concealment from marauding bands.

He climbed the slope to the top of the meadow and lay down, face to the sky. Hunger rolled noisily in his stomach, but he decided to hold off eating his apple and sandwich. The sound of running water brought him upright. The stream ran clear and spar-kling and, suddenly thirsty, he filled his cupped hands and brought them to his mouth, remembering in the nick of time it wasn't safe to drink just any water.

Even in this idyllic spot PCBs abounded, pollution was everywhere. Angered by his own action, he let the water trickle back through his fingers.

He lay down again and closed his eyes. Perhaps, at this very minute, a princess was climbing the hill, silken garments blown by the wind, golden hair flying, tiny feet encased in velvet slippers. Feet again? He and Liszt were both foot fetishists. There were worse kinds. And she would have a voice like jewels dropped into a satin bag! He could hardly wait! A bee buzzed him. He blew it away. Birds sang. The sun lulled him. It was Walt Disney all the way.

Then he felt eyes on him. The princess! He believed in miracles. Quivering with anticipation, he waited for her soft lips to land on his. He couldn't expect any soul kissing, not on the first go-round.

Nothing moved, nothing happened. Yet someone was standing over him. He opened his eyes the merest crack. *That* was a princess? What did he know? It was his first princess, after all. Disguised as a raggedy waif with snarled hair and skinny arms and legs that looked too long for the rest of her.

"My daddy says you don't get off our proppity," said the waif in a penetrating voice, "he's gonna shoot." Some jewels.

He sat up and looked at his watch, giving himself time to regroup. He waited for her to smile. But she remained stony faced and unblinking.

"It's about time I was going anyway," he said, calling her bluff. Behind him came the sound of someone large crashing through the underbrush. Hastily, he stood up.

"I wasn't doing anything," he said. The child's eyes flickered. He thought he heard heavy breathing as the crashing sounds grew closer. He started down the hill.

"He scatted fast!" the waif hollered. "Lookit him go!" As he ran, he tried to remember the exact spot in which he'd buried his bike. Suppose it was gone? Suppose the marauders had seen him conceal it and, the minute his back was turned, they'd stolen it?

It was there, where he'd left it. He hoisted it hurriedly over the stone wall and, poised to take off, he looked back. A man stood there, shaking one fist, the other filled with a gun. Shouting obscenities.

He assumed a racer's crouch, making himself small, as small as possible, in case the guy decided to let go at him.

Again, he rode as if demons were pursuing him. He would not have been surprised to have a car pull alongside, to have the man behind the wheel instruct him to get inside because he was wanted for questioning.

I didn't even drink his water, for Pete's sake. Tim's morning, which had started off so well, had been trashed, ruined, thrown on the ash heap. The trip back seemed endless. The sun had lost its warmth, though it was close to noon.

"Your father was here," his mother said when he got home. "He said you had a date with him and Joy to drive golf balls. You didn't leave a note, Tim. I was worried. I told him I didn't know where you'd gone." Her face was wan.

"Oh, God, I forgot," he said. "I biked a long way out of town and found this meadow. You wouldn't believe how beautiful it was, Mom." A catch in his throat stopped him. How to tell her how wonderful the place had been, how high his expectations. There was no way. "Then this little kid told me to get out or else her father'd shoot me. This creep came at me with a gun." He shouldn't tell her this. It would only add fuel to the worry fire constantly simmering in her head. "How come? I want to know," he plunged on, unable to stop, "if I was such a monster, why did he send his little kid up instead of coming himself? How come?"

To his great dismay, he felt tears building. He turned his back, fighting for control. It was not a situation that called for tears but they were there.

"Oh, Tim." His mother's voice was gentle. "How terrible. You're sure you didn't do anything to antagonize him? You know how short people's fuses are these days."

"I swear, Ma. I didn't even drink any of his lousy

old water. I was just lying there, thinking about things, enjoying myself. It's crazy. Absolutely crazy."

He heard her move behind him and hoped she wouldn't touch him. Not now. Give me time, he thought.

"I was just heating up some soup," she said in a normal voice. "Want some?"

"Not right now, thanks. I'd better ride over to the driving range and try to catch Dad. I feel bad about not being here. I want to explain."

He thought, and did not say, I wouldn't want him to think I skinned out on purpose.

"And Melissa called." His mother put the crowning touch on his day, without knowing she did so. "She said to come over about three-thirty tomorrow. Her mother will drive you to the dance, she said."

He hadn't told his mother about the tea dance and Melissa. He could hear the question in her voice but she didn't ask.

"Oh, God." He groaned. "Maybe it would've been better if that creep had let me have it after all. Just a flesh wound. Just enough to put me out of commission for a couple of days."

He heard his mother draw in her breath sharply, but he didn't look at her. "I'll be back in about an hour, Ma," he said, and climbed on his bike once more.

Chapter 14

On Sunday, he went to ten o'clock Mass, seeking solace. Church didn't always offer solace but he went anyway, always hopeful. He sat in one of the back pews so he could watch people come in, watch the way they genuflected before entering the pews. The older the people were, he noticed, the more they sort of bobbed up and down gently before they settled in with their rosary beads. They managed never to hit the floor with their knees, only grazing it. Arthritis, probably. His grandmother had arthritis in her left knee and she said it wasn't any fun. He'd suffered a torn cartilage while playing soccer, so he appreciated what a wacko knee was like. He liked the way light hit the stained-glass windows, sending shafts of color spraying over the congregation. He liked the way the church smelled, a mixture of incense and the flowers that decorated the altar. He kept a close eye on the altar boys, checking to make sure they knew all the right moves. He and Patrick had each had a turn at being altar boys. Now, he'd heard, they had girls as altar boys in some parishes. Boy, the world she is a-changin'.

Sometimes, even at his advanced age, he still felt an overpowering urge to laugh that hit him only in church. He didn't know why. The desire had been more acute when he'd been four or five and new to the ways of the world. He remembered thrashing around in the pew, restless, not sure why he was here in the first place. He'd checked out the missals tucked in the rack, checked out the people sitting in front of him, and wanted to touch those people with one finger, as light as a spider. He had envied kids he saw surrounded by siblings, all of them in their Sunday best, their faces shiny with soap, their clothes crisp and new. He remembered watching them wistfully, the families of five, maybe six or more, kids, watching while the parents carefully spaced the kids, inserting themselves between the ones more apt to fight with each other, making warning faces at the livelier ones, telling them to behave. It was then, and only then, he regretted being an only child. Most of the time, he thought it was fine.

He could always tell the parochial-school kids from the ones who went to public school. The parochial-school kids were much better behaved, and when they went up to receive communion, their hands were always neatly folded, with the fingers interlocking, their eyes cast down, and they didn't chew the host the way the public-school kids did.

This morning a little kid of about two sat in front of him, trying to stare him down. The kid wore Oshkosh overalls and a red baseball cap, and had the most unblinking stare he'd ever seen. He tried making a couple of funny faces, hoping to break the kid up. No luck. The little weasel didn't know how to smile.

The sermon lasted twenty-one minutes. He timed it. Each time Father McDuff paused to collect his thoughts, he thought for sure it was over. Then the priest got his second wind and plunged onward, always onward. An old nun had just died. Father McDuff said she was a very holy woman, a member of a cloistered order who never left her cell, never went beyond the walls of the convent. She spent her days praying. She had loved God and man, the priest said. She was filled with love. He wondered why the old nun had never gone out into the world to tend to the sick, the needy, and the poor, who needed all the help they could get. If she had, she would have been using her love to the greatest advantage. Or so it seemed to him.

"And now will you please offer one another the sign of peace?" Father McDuff asked. This was the part he hated. He came to church to be alone with his thoughts, not to shake hands with total strangers. Once, he'd tried standing with his arms crossed on his chest, looking straight ahead, pretending he was deaf and/or dumb. But an old lady with a tipsy hat crouching on her blue hair had given him a nudge with her sharp elbow and said in a bossy way, "Shake hands, young man. I don't like it any better than you do, but shake hands, if you please. The sign of peace, if you please." She looked like a troublemaker, so he did as she instructed him. From that time on, he didn't fight it. He shook hands with every Tom, Dick, and Harry anxious to be in on the peace giving, even if the guy might go home after church and kick the dog down the stairs for laying a couple of turds on the new rug.

"Peace be with you," he said. He shook hands to the left of him, to the right of him, and when he grabbed the little kid's hand and shook it, the kid let out a startled yelp and burst into tears. The mother shot him a baleful glance as she soothed her baby, probably thinking he'd stuck the kid with a pin. Or with a machete he happened to keep in his pocket.

To escape her indignant gaze, he turned to shake hands with whoever was behind him.

"Peace be with you," he said.

Sophie! It was Sophie, hand out, a bemused smile on her face. He grinned and shook her hand so long she pulled it away from him, as if anxious to have it back. It was the first time he'd touched her. Her skin felt hot and dry. He felt the blood rush to his ears, warming them, turning them bright, the same color as a maple leaf when the frost hits it. He turned back to face the altar, flustered, heart pumping violently. He tingled all over. Sophie at St. Raymond's! Wonders will never cease.

Pull yourself together, he told himself sternly. Now's your chance. Church was a nice neutral ground, unlike school. When Mass ended, he skinned out fast and got his bike from the rack in the parking lot to push it around to the front where people mingled, gossiping cheerfully, giving Father McDuff compliments on his too-long sermon. He didn't really think Sophie would still be there but she was, standing in a group of girls.

He walked slowly in her direction, pushing his bike. When he looked at her, she was looking back at him.

"I didn't know you went to St. Raymond's," he said, starting the conversation off in a brilliant manner.

"I don't. I'm here with a friend."

"Well," he said. Pause. "How'd you like the sermon?"

Sophie met that head on, her expression aloof, eyes wary.

Please God, he prayed, I need help. Put some clever words in my mouth and I'll follow you anywhere, God.

But Sophie had turned back to continue the conversation he'd obviously interrupted, as if she hadn't heard him, or, if she had heard him, hadn't understood.

"You know my father," she said, rolling her eyes. The girls she was talking to laughed and rolled their eyes back. "He went around yelling that he was calling the cops if I got any more letters like that one. I don't know what he thinks the cops can do. Probably stake out the post office or something dumb like that." Sophie threw the crowd into stitches with that one.

Tim was pretty busy with his dialogue with God and didn't really take in what Sophie had said, until he thought about it later.

Please God, if you make me look good now, I'll owe you one, he was thinking.

"What'd the letter say anyway?" a girl asked. "I mean, what was so bad about it?"

Sophie shrugged. "It was kind of weird. I mean, it was just sort of crazy. Full of words I didn't understand, old-fashioned stuff. Things people don't say these days. If you know what I mean."

Her friends' faces remained blank. Obviously they didn't know what she meant.

"I couldn't tell if the person who wrote it was serious or just pulling my leg, you know?"

Sophie shook her head. "But, I don't know. Every time I read it, I feel different. Like it's weird one time, then the next it's sort of, I don't know, sort of grabby. It grabs me. Just when I start getting mad, something makes me hang in there, waiting for what's coming next. Then I get mad again."

Now he was frozen to the spot he stood upon, a dopey smile on his face. Letting her words sink in.

"You'd have to read it to know what I'm talking about," Sophie continued. "I'll bring it to school tomorrow to show it to you all. That is, if my father hasn't taken it to the police station so they can check it for fingerprints."

Collective peals of laughter were so uproarious, people turned to stare, wondering what was so funny.

Fingerprints! Boy, lucky thing he'd worn his mother's gloves. It just showed it paid to be careful. There was no way they could trace that letter to him. Unless they grilled the friendly postman he'd given it to. Would the postman remember him? Upon cross-examination, would he knit his brow and say, "Well, there was this kind of weird-looking kid who told me he didn't want her to know who sent the letter. Kind of a criminal type he was, now that I think about it."

Would that happen? No. Impossible. He had a forgettable face, didn't he? Besides, what crime had he committed? None.

A big white car pulled up and Sophie and her pals got in. She didn't even say good-bye.

Chapter 15

Traveling on foot, he took the long way around to
Patrick's. He didn't want to get where he was going
any sooner than he could help. He was a bundle of
nerves, as a direct result of this morning's meeting
with Sophie, as well as the prospect of escorting Melissa to the tea dance at St. Raymond's.

"What on earth happened to you?" his mother had
inquired when he'd arrived home from church. "You
look as if you'd been through the mill."

He told her of Father McDuff's sermon about the
cloistered nun, said he'd run into some girls he knew,
neither of which explained his appearance, which was
that of someone who'd just had an unforgettable experience. An epiphany.

His mother had insisted he wear his church clothes

to the dance—shirt, tie, even matching socks. He left his glasses in his bureau, deciding they'd only gild the lily. He walked at a snail's pace, giving the neighbors a treat. So, Sophie had received his letter, and thought it was grabby! Once he really got into it, this writing of love letters would turn out to be a cinch. He felt it in his bones. With a little practice, he would hit his stride, like a highly trained athlete who knows how to pace himself, or herself, who knows how to breathe properly so there would always be breath for the task ahead. Knows all the tricks that add up to winning. Coming in first.

For that was what he had in mind—coming in first with Sophie. The first hurdle had been passed. Three cheers for the mailman. That mailman was a veritable Cupid. Just for the price of a postage stamp, he, Timothy J. Owen, was starting a whole new phase of his heretofore dull and dreary life. *The Love Song of J. Alfred Prufrock*, by T. S. Eliot, first read by him at age thirteen, had made an indelible impression. From then on, he thought of himself as J. Timothy Owen, a name to conjure with. That little old stamp tucked up there in the corner of the envelope had started a chain of events that could lead almost anywhere. It was awesome, what one stamp could do, could lead to. Romance, adventure, intrigue. It was enough to make the mind boggle, thinking about the power of a stamp, of a mailman to bring about a radical change in someone's existence. He vowed that if he got out of this tea dance alive, he'd give the mailman a tip at Christmas to thank him for the superior job he'd done.

But, even taking the long way, he got where he was going eventually. As he turned the corner that led to Patrick's street, he saw a figure on the sidewalk, eyes shaded, scanning the horizon. It was Melissa, on the lookout. He waved and the figure scooted out of sight. All was serene as he pulled into the front yard. He thought he saw the curtains move. Melissa was watching. He knocked on the door very softly. Maybe she wouldn't hear his knock and he could go home and claim he'd been there but they'd all gone somewhere else.

The door flew open.

"Hello, Tim," Melissa said, blushing. She was resplendent in a shocking-pink sweater and black leather jacket with three earrings in each ear. Wild. Her eyelids were decidedly lavender. Patrick's mother would lower the boom on that eyeshadow, he figured.

"Come on in." He followed Melissa inside and thought she seemed unsteady on her feet. She wore stockings and heels. That was it. She had to get her sea legs before she could walk on those heels.

Solemnly they sat down, he on the couch, Melissa

on a chair across the room. "My mother will be right down," Melissa said. "She's taking us."

"I know," he said. He glanced around surreptitiously, expecting Patrick to pounce out at him.

"Where's Patrick?" he asked at last. "We could shoot a little pool while we're waiting."

"Patrick's gone to my aunt and uncle's for Sunday dinner," Melissa announced, lips tucked into a shadow of her former mouth.

"Oh." So Patrick had been shanghaied, sent to the bush leagues, and was even at this moment scarfing down prime ribs *au jus* and Yorkshire pudding. Poor Patrick.

A heavy silence fell. Into it he spoke.

"So, Melissa, what're you up to this summer?"

Melissa cleared her throat and inched to the edge of her chair.

"I'm writing a novel," she said in a little breathless voice. "I'm entering it in a contest for hitherto unpublished authors under the age of twenty-one. The first prize is a thousand dollars advance against publication, and after they publish your novel, you get royalties, which means they pay you a certain amount for each copy that's sold." She had obviously memorized every word. "Plus, my novel has to be between thirty-five and fifty thousand words."

"That's a lot of words," he said after a bit.

"I've had a couple of poems published in our class paper," Melissa confessed, "but I don't think they count. Anyway . . ." She eyed him defiantly. "I'm not going to mention them."

"Good plan," he said. "What's it about?"

"My novel?" She eyed him, and he was tempted to say, "Wasn't that what we were talking about?" and did not.

"Well, it's about this sixteen-year-old girl who has a terrible fight with her mother, so she runs away from home and hitches a ride with this guy. He is a real hunk with blond hair and a really good build, and he looks like a preppy, but it turns out he's into hard drugs and he plays in a rock band and everything."

Melissa stopped. He knew he should say something so he said, "Sounds good. What happens?"

"I have to work out that part, the rest of it," Melissa said. "I've got several ideas but I have to work it out."

Patrick's mother came in and he leaped to his feet with such alacrity he almost knocked her over.

"You both look so nice," she said. "Could you give me a hand, Tim? I have a lot of cupcakes and sandwiches to put in the car. I'm the refreshments chairwoman and, without me, they don't eat. Why don't you stay put, Missy? Tim and I can manage." Melissa ducked behind the comics and he and Mrs. Scanlon went to the kitchen to get the supplies. He followed her into the garage, loaded with boxes.

116

"Tim, you're a darling." Mrs. Scanlon surveyed the packing job. "She would've been so crushed if you'd turned her down. I thank you for your kindness." Mrs. Scanlon leaned over and kissed his cheek.

He took it in stride. "That's OK," he said. Sir Lancelot on the prowl, that was him.

All three of them sat in the front seat. He was willing to sit in back, but Mrs. Scanlon said there was plenty of room. He and Melissa sat rigid, arms at sides, careful not to touch each other, as Mrs. Scanlon drove them to the tea dance.

The parking lot at St. Raymond's was filled with eighth graders, all dressed up and running in circles like crazies. As he helped Mrs. Scanlon unload the goodies and carry them inside, he felt very old. In eighth grade, he remembered, it had been possible to be turned on by the thought of plenty of cupcakes, egg-salad sandwiches, and punch. Extraordinary, but true. It was only with the pressure of added years and experience that one realized food wasn't everything in life.

"Hey, Tim O.!" He knew immediately that mocking voice. No one else called him Tim O.

Tony Montaldo approached with both arms held high like a politician seeking votes. "Never thought I'd see an old geezer like you at St. Raymond's eighth-grade bash." Tony's teeth gleamed in a malicious smile.

Tim scarcely raised his head from the task of stack-

117

ing the tall piles of boxes before taking them inside. Now he knew for sure this was going to be a bummer. Tony Montaldo was the icing on the cake.

"These are the times that try men's souls. Tyranny, like hell, is not easily conquered." Thomas Paine, a supremely eloquent man, spoke to him again. His soul was being sorely tried, and Tony Montaldo was the tyrant.

Melissa, meanwhile, talked animatedly to a group of girls who stole looks in his direction every so often and when he caught them looking at him they turned back into their circle, their voices rising shrilly as they undoubtedly discussed world affairs, waiting for the festivities to commence.

"I only came for the grub," Tony bragged. "My sister's at St. Raymond's, and she said the grub was going to be good so I decided to come and eat."

"I guess that about does it," Patrick's mother said, looking at her watch. "It's almost four, Tim." She smiled at him encouragingly and he thought she knew how he was feeling. He followed her into St. Raymond's, with Melissa and her coterie of buddies bringing up the rear.

The gym smelled the way he remembered it smelling. You couldn't do much to change that smell, one of good old-fashioned sweat. No matter how old you got to be, how much water had gone over the dam

118

or under the bridge, gyms smelled like gyms. In a way, it was reassuring. If, in yet another reincarnation, he or Patrick came back to St. Raymond's gym, say in the twenty-first century, they'd know immediately where they were.

One of the mothers was messing with the stereo. He couldn't stand it when mothers messed with stuff like stereos. They always loused it up. The music blasted suddenly, mowing everything in its path. It was that singer with the frizzy hair and dangly earrings. He didn't think much of her but he was in the minority. A lot of the girls here today had frizzy hair and dangly earrings, in an obvious attempt to resemble the singer, whose name escaped him. He thought they looked like woodland creatures, peering out from behind the underbrush of their hair. On the other hand, he himself was no slouch in the bangs department. Protective instincts, he figured. Everybody needs something to hide behind.

Melissa, who had been standing by the refreshment table, came to stand next to him. He tensed, waiting for the music, wondering what he'd do when it began. Someone turned down the sound. The mothers looked relieved. They didn't understand the louder the better.

"All right! Kids! Please! Quiet!" The mother shouting at them was obviously the head honcho. She clapped her hands together for order, and went on clapping long after silence had fallen.

"Our first dance is going to be a change-partners dance." The mother smiled around at them as if she'd just said something witty. "When the music stops, I want all of you to change partners with the couple nearest you. That way we'll all get to know one another, and we're going to make this the best tea dance ever at St. Raymond's!" Like Liszt, she dealt in exclamation points.

He tightened his stomach muscles, as if for a blow, and grasped Melissa firmly as she put her hand on his shoulder tentatively, as if testing it for doneness. Gingerly, they clasped hands and moved their feet. Melissa kept looking down.

"Keep moving," he whispered fiercely. "And look at me. It doesn't do any good to look at your feet."

In a moment of panic, his muscles locked, and he thought wildly, I'm paralyzed. Then Melissa backed away and he followed her. Once started, he found if he kept a firm grip on her, and he didn't look down, he was all right. It was like being on the top of the Empire State Building. If he didn't look down, he was all right.

For a split second, she raised her head and he saw the terrified expression on her face and felt better. She was in worse shape than he was. His mother had read a book called *I'm Dancing as Fast as I Can*, which perfectly described the way he felt. He was dancing as fast as he could.

"Relax," he said. "Nobody's going to shoot you."

She gave a nervous little laugh. "I always have to go to the bathroom when I'm nervous," she said. Then, realizing what she'd said, a stricken look replaced the terrified one.

"Me, too," he said, and they both laughed.

The music stopped. Melissa's hand dropped from his shoulder. They were supposed to change partners. A big girl in a fussy dress caught his eye. She was alone and trying to look as if she didn't care. He would rescue her from her plight, a gallant thing to do, he thought. He strode toward her and a long leg came from out of nowhere and tripped him. He sprawled flat on his face on the floor of St. Raymond's gym.

"Sorry about that, Tim O." Tony Montaldo grinned down at him. "Didn't see you in time." Tony helped him up, brushed him off, and whispered in his ear, "Figured you needed an excuse to get out of dancing with another fat broad. You go from one fat one to another, eh, Tim O.?"

That did it. Tim took a long breath, drew back, and punched Tony in the face. Right in between Tony's mouth and nose. It was a most satisfying feeling, almost as good as hitting a golf ball just right. He stood back and watched the blood drip from Tony's nose. With any luck at all, he might've loosened a couple of Tony's beautiful teeth, too.

"Fight! Fight!" voices shouted excitedly. Nothing like a good fight to liven up a tea dance.

"What on earth is going on here?" The head-honcho mother steamed up, scarlet with indignation. Tony didn't try to hit back—he was too busy plugging up his nose. "This is a social occasion, boys. I expect you to behave like gentlemen."

He saw Melissa's white face and felt bad. But, when he looked at Tony's face, a great joy seized him. Whatever happened next, it would be worth it. Even if they strung him up by his thumbs, it would be worth it.

"Tim, why don't you go out and get a breath of air? It's all right. Things will settle down." Mrs. Scanlon spoke softly. "Come back when you feel better."

Hands in pockets to show he didn't care, he sauntered out to the hall, as she'd suggested. What he really wanted to do was just split the whole scene. His feeling of exhilaration had subsided, and one of humiliation took its place. He bent down for a drink of water from the drinking fountain.

"Hello, Tim." Sister Mary Teresa didn't seem surprised to see him. She didn't mention the brawl. Maybe she hadn't seen it. "I thought I recognized you, though you've grown some. How are you? I hadn't seen you around, so I thought perhaps you'd moved."

"No, I'm still here, Sister." She meant she hadn't seen him at Mass. He only went when the spirit moved him. His father was Catholic, or had been until the divorce.

Without warning his voice trembled, and he bent to take another long drink to give himself time to recover. Sister Mary Teresa waited patiently for him to finish.

"You probably will be surprised to hear it, Sister," he said, on impulse, "but lately I've been thinking about souls. Not only mine, but souls in general."

Sister Mary Teresa nodded and waited for what he'd say next, her eyes bright with curiosity. Nothing had ever surprised her, he remembered now.

"Well, to tell the truth, I've been reading a book of famous love letters, and I noticed how frequently they talked about the soul back then, Sister, and that made me think of you."

She laughed. "That's interesting, Tim. I don't think I'm usually associated with love letters."

"Well, you taught us about souls. And I got to thinking. If I could see my soul, which I know I can't, I wonder what it would look like. And I decided it might be like a laser beam. Sort of a darting light." He paused, out of breath, and waited for her reaction. Two girls walked by, looked back at him, and whispered to each other.

She said nothing. "What do you think of that, Sister? Do you think that's sacrilegious? I don't mean it to be. I'm only trying to relate the soul to everyday life, trying to equate it with something. I mean, if you don't have faith enough to believe in the soul, maybe you would have faith if you were able to liken it to something modern. Get it?"

"If it makes you feel better to do so, Tim, if it makes you think about God, well, I say go for it. I don't think God would mind. He might even approve. How's Patrick?"

"He's fine. I brought his sister to the dance. She asked me, and I came anyway, even though I'm much too old for it. Her name's Melissa." He found talking to Sister Mary Teresa calming, so that he forgot for a minute his embarrassment and anger.

"Oh, I know Melissa. The Scanlons are a fine family. Well, Tim"— Sister Mary Teresa put out her hand— "it was very nice to see you after all this time. If you ever want to discuss souls again, come by. I'm always here, and I'd be glad to see you." They shook hands and he watched her walk down the hall and disappear.

When he went back to the gym, Melissa was standing off to one side, looking somewhat forlorn. He walked toward her. When she saw him, she looked relieved. "I'm sorry, Melissa," he said. "I couldn't help myself. He tripped me."

"Oh, I thought maybe you'd left—gone home, that

is. You know?" She smiled. "It's all right, Tim. He had it coming."

The music started up and, as they moved out onto the gym floor, she peered up at him and said, "You look different without your glasses."

This dancing routine was easier the second time around. He steered her confidently around the other dancers. "I don't really need them," he said. "They're not prescription. I only wear them because they make me look like a scholar. I want people to think I'm an intellectual. They're fake." He'd never told anyone that before, not even Patrick, though he knew Patrick suspected.

"Oh," said Melissa. "Well, anyway, you look nice without them. You look nice with them, too. I didn't mean that." She smiled self-consciously and tightened her grip on his hand. "I think this is the best dance ever. Are you having a good time, Tim?"

"It's the best tea dance I've ever been to," he said.

"Have you been to lots of tea dances before?"

"No," he said, "this is my first one."

She giggled. "Oh Tim, you're *so* funny."

When he thought about it, he *was* pretty funny. He began to hum, keeping time to the music.

Chapter 16

"How was it?" his mother asked.

"Not bad. Not as bad as I'd thought it would be."
Worse.

"Almost nothing is," she replied.

Little did she know. He'd tell her in his own good
time. Not now.

"I saw Sister Mary Teresa, Ma. We had a nice conversation."

"How is Sister MT?" His mother had always called
her that. "What's she up to?"

"Same old stuff. We talked about souls. I told her
what I thought about my soul and she said she didn't
think God would mind."

"She probably thought it was a step in the right
direction that you're even thinking about your soul,"

his mother said. "Sister MT always was a liberated woman. If she hadn't become a nun, she might've been a stateswoman or a politician. Or maybe the president of a college. A very far-thinking woman. I'm glad you ran into her, Tim. I bet she was glad to see you, too."

"Yeah, I think she was. She remembered me. I was kind of surprised. Although I guess I gave her so much grief she probably couldn't forget me. She asked about Patrick, too. How'd your day go?" he thought to ask.

"Kev was here," she said. "We went over the books, and it turns out we barely made the rent money last month. It's very discouraging. If we had a better location, we'd sell more, and also command better prices. But we can't afford the rents on Main Street, so we'll have to stay tucked away in the alley." His mother was clearly disturbed. "Kev's not sure he wants to continue in the antique business." She busied herself arranging a pile of books and magazines, keeping herself occupied. "He thinks he might like to head west, to Oregon or Washington State, something like that. He wants me to go with him."

He took off his jacket and felt his armpits. "Boy, did I ever work up a sweat," he said, pleased with himself. "Dancing is a lot of work. Even the kind of dancing I do, which isn't exactly what Fred Astaire had in mind. Melissa and I were about even, I'd say. She looked at her feet a lot. She might be a star tap

127

dancer, but when it comes to touch dancing, she isn't any better than I am." He loosened his tie and sat down. "What did you tell him? Are you going?" A picture of his mother and Kev wrapped in each other's arms in the orange tent flitted briefly through his head. "Are you getting married?" With an effort he remained nonchalant and noncommittal, waiting for her answer.

"I don't think Kev has marriage in mind." His mother's face was turned away from him, but he heard the quaver in her voice. "He wants me to go with him on a trial basis."

"Who's on trial?"

His mother laughed without mirth. "Me, I guess."

Oh, boy. If Kev turned up now, he'd smash in his face, punch him out good. He'd get him in a shoulder lock and grind him down to pulp. He'd set the monsters on Kev and tell them they had *carte blanche*. Do your darndest, kids, he'd say. And the monsters would lead Kev away and that would be the end of him. A little taste of blood was a dangerous thing, he thought.

"That guy is something else, Ma." He shook his head. "You're well rid of him, if you ask me." Which she hadn't.

His mother frowned and chewed on her lip. "Does it seem extraordinary to you, Tim, that you and I are talking to each other this way? I mean, it's as if you're

128

my contemporary and I came to you for advice. And you're my son, my sixteen-year-old son." She got up and went out to the kitchen. Presently, he heard the kettle singing, sounding off. She was making tea. She always made tea in a crisis.

"You want to know what I think?" She stood in the doorway, cup in hand. "I think the trend of parents becoming more their children's contemporaries than their parents is a bad thing. I think children are forced into adult situations at a ridiculously early age. Here we are, Tim, talking like this. I wouldn't have had this happen to us for all the world. I am your mother. You should be coming to me for advice, not the other way around. I'm supposed to show you the way, protect you, teach you how to cope with life. Now our roles seem to be reversed. It's nutty. Absolutely nutty."

"Ma, I need lots of advice," he said. "You and Dad always taught me to think for myself, to work out my own problems. That's what I try to do, but it doesn't always work that way. Stuff piles up. There's a lot going on out there that's bad. We both know that. You're a good mother. So you got tied up with a wimp. That could happen to anybody."

She blinked rapidly several times and drank her tea. He thought it would burn her mouth, she gulped it down so fast.

"If you want to keep going in the antique business, well, keep going. Things will improve. You'll make some big bucks if you try. You don't need Kev. Go it alone. I'll help. Dad will want to help, too, I'll bet."

The cup rattled in the saucer as she set them down. "I don't want Dad to know anything about this, Tim. That's understood. This is between you and me."

"Whoa." He held up his hand. "I didn't say I was going to tell Dad anything. All I said was he'd probably help if he knew you needed it. That's all. My lips are sealed, Ma."

She calmed down. "OK, I'll see how it goes. Thanks, Tim. Would you like a cup of tea?"

"No, thanks. I swilled down enough punch to float a battleship. I'm going to change my duds, get out of these party clothes, and write a letter."

"I can't get over you." His mother shook her head, smiling at him. "One minute it's like pulling teeth to get you to write a thank-you note to your grandparents, and next, you're borrowing stamps and firing off letters all over the place. What gives?"

"Ma, you have your secrets, I have mine. I'll let you in on mine someday when we're both older and wiser, OK?"

"Fair enough."

"What smells so good?"

"Turkey. It was on special, seventy-nine cents a

pound. I couldn't resist. We'll probably be eating it for weeks, though."

Maybe this would be the moment for him to tell her about his recipe for Turkey Kev. Now that Kev was a has-been. Still, he didn't tell her, not wanting to count his turkeys too soon.

On his way to his room, he heard the telephone. When he picked up the upstairs extension, his mother said, "It's Patrick," and hung up.

"Hello, fool," said Patrick.

"Did you say that when my mother answered?" he asked.

"Yeah. Sometimes I get caught with my pants down," Patrick admitted.

"What'd she say?"

"She said, 'You must have the wrong number. There are no fools here.' Then you got on. Tell your mother I'm sorry. Tell her that if I'd known she was going to answer, I never would've said that. How was it?"

"How was what?" He'd let Patrick dangle a while.

"The dance, clown. The orgy at St. Raymond's. Melissa said it was peachy, but you know how girls exaggerate. Melissa also said you punched out Tony Montaldo. About time somebody did."

"Yeah," he said. "I saw Sister Mary Teresa. She wanted to know if you were still pushing a broom somewhere, or if you had become a junior executive.

I told her you were maturing, but slowly, very slowly."

"No kidding?" Patrick sounded very pleased. "She asked about me, huh? Well, whadya know."

"Patrick, I have to split. I've got a big problem I have to work out. See you in the A.M., all right?"

"Not if I see you first," Patrick said. "As far as your problem goes, I accept house calls. But not after midnight. *Ciao*."

Chapter 17

He picked up where he'd left off.

"Have your affections cooled?"

What affections? Something like a sharp stab of pain struck near his heart as it occurred to him it was quite possible Sophie's heart belonged to another. Someone who was undoubtedly tall and strong and good-looking. Someone who was also a good athlete, good dancer, and all-around jock. That was the type she'd go for. He could tell. Too late, he could tell.

Maybe it was somebody in the school band, someone she saw every day, with whom she had much in common. This cat would play sweet music and, as Sophie swayed gently like a snake charmer, blowing on her oboe (for he'd seen her, stealing into band practice more than once), this guy would play the drums. The drums were what he'd be best at, although maybe he also played piano and the French horn. But it was the drums he starred at, playing them aggressively, with a jungle beat that stirred a caldron of emotions. Without this guy, the entire orchestra would collapse. This guy of Sophie's was a golden boy. Make no mistake.

He groaned and rested his head in his hands. What good would anonymous love letters do against such an adversary? Probably the golden boy composed drum solos, which he dedicated to Sophie, solos without words, as it would be next to impossible even for this paragon to write words to a drum solo. All that pounding, that jungle beat, would get to her, though, and win her heart more surely than any love letter, anonymous or not.

Still, he wasn't giving up that easy. Hang in there, he told himself, gritting his teeth. Faint heart never won nothing. Isn't that what his little voice told him again and again?

"Ah, Sophie, I beseech you, do not be ashamed of a friend you once favored. Have you not taken possession of me? Think of those times of happiness that, to my torture, I shall never forget. Look what I was and what I am now. How often was not your heart, filled with love for another, touched by the passion of mine?"

There he was again, the little drummer boy.

"Nothing in the world is sweeter than you." That last line was his own. Nothing earthshaking about it, but just straight talk. Like dancing, the second time around in the letter department was also easier. Briskly, with a flourish, he signed his trademark, "Yours, Anon.," and slipped his missive into an envelope, barehanded. Let the fingerprints fall where they might.

It was odd that writing those letters, largely made up of other people's words, served to put words of his own into his head. He lay back and began yet another letter to Sophie in his head.

"I long to see you again. To embrace you, to look into your eyes, eyes of silence and melancholy, which render you even more mine. I want to be alone with you in some sunlit meadow, kid, your hand in mine."

That was his meadow, flower studded, disturbed only by a sparkling stream, where the air was clear and the sun shone and the birds sang. And his dream princess turned out to be a narrow-boned, homely little waif masquerading as a princess with a voice like a chain saw, whose daddy came at him with a gun.

There was real life and there was imaginary. And never the twain shall meet.

His mother tapped on his door. "It's Dad, for you," she said, poking in her head.

"Tim, how about attacking a bucket of balls again this Saturday? Maybe we'll have better luck this time."

"Sure, Dad. And this time I won't crump out on you. I'm really sorry about that."

"No harm done. Glad you can make it. See you about ten, then, on Saturday."

During the week he helped his mother after school. She had taken a booth at the antique show to be held at the high school on the weekend. "Fifty Dealers, Fifty!" boasted the signs posted in every shop window and on every telephone pole. As if Fifty Dealers, Fifty made the show special.

"Kev called," she said when he got home after school on Friday. "He says he heard about a shop that may be available at the end of June. The location is perfect. Of course, the rent's high but Kev says the new place would probably triple our business."

"I thought he was on his way out west to go white-water rafting, or something," he said, keeping his voice light.

"He hasn't decided. Would you get me more of that plastic-wrap stuff, darling? It's in the kitchen."

Sophie must have gotten the second letter by now. He had mailed it three days ago, and was working on a third. He followed the same procedure he had before, keeping a close watch on her to see what, if any, emotions might cross her face when she saw him. He had thought the meeting at Mass might have cemented their relationship. She gave him no sign. Her eyes were as wary as before, her expression as aloof. He wondered what he could do to rouse some emotion in her. Or was she seething quietly inside, waiting for him to make some sort of move?

He planned to slip into the auditorium to watch her at band practice. The sight of Sophie swaying in time to her oboe music moved him beyond words. But a self-important senior, of whom there seemed to be many, stood guard, arms akimbo, legs apart, a regular SS type.

"No non-band members allowed in," the senior stated, scowling.

"I'm doing a story for the local paper," he said, peering nearsightedly from behind his nonprescription glasses, looking, he thought, as rumpled, as scholarly, and as intellectual as any college don. He carried a notebook and a pencil, which he whipped out and held at the ready, lending a touch of verisimilitude to his claim of being a reporter. "We're doing a rundown on school bands in the area," he said, acting very cool. "May even do a Sunday feature."

"Back off, baby." Evidently the senior was smarter than he looked. "You'll have to clear it with the authorities."

What a troglodyte.

"What is this, *1984* all over again?"

The senior sneered and turned away. Tim skulked outside, thinking he might catch Sophie on her way out. He would walk with her, maybe even hold her hand, her hot, dry hand, which he had shaken as a sign of peace. Surely that was a bond between them. Had she gotten his letter, or had the mailman been derelict in his duty, pausing perhaps, at a local video-game emporium for a couple of games, thereby delaying its delivery? He thought he heard the clear, pure notes of Sophie's oboe rising above the cacophony of all the other instruments. But he couldn't be sure.

What had he done before he started writing love letters to Sophie? He couldn't remember.

Perhaps she was ill, he thought, as the band members filed out and she wasn't among them. Perhaps she was lying even now, at this moment, in a delirious state, asking for him over and over. Her parents bending solicitously over the sickbed, perplexed at her reiteration of, "Anon, I want Anon. I will never get well if I do not see my dear Anon."

The parents, brows knitted, would clutch each other and whisper, "Who is this Anon our daughter seeks?"

Who indeed.

Chapter 18

Saturday morning he was out on the sidewalk, waiting, when his father pulled up. Alone. Yeh.

"Joy had some errands to run. She'll meet us there," his father said.

"Dad, what say we play tennis next week? You think Joy'll let you off the hook for once?"

His father, always a careful driver, kept his eyes on the road.

"I thought you'd enjoyed hitting golf balls, Tim," his father spoke at last. "It's not a question of being 'on the hook,' as you put it."

Once again, he'd put his foot in it.

"Sorry, Dad. I only meant I'd like to play tennis with you once in a while. I have a feeling golf isn't my sport."

"You haven't given it a chance, Tim. I know it's discouraging, but you'll see that time and practice will improve your game."

"That's just it. I'd like to try a game instead of this just hitting the balls. If we played an actual game, I might get with it."

"You have a point. We'll play next week. Either at Joy's club, or we can try the nine-holer here, at the driving range."

They hung around, waiting for Joy to show. "Len Feeley must be off his feed this morning," his father said. "He usually comes out to say hello." They could see him inside his office, pacing, once in a while pressing his nose against the glass to see how things were going.

They waited for quite a while. His father took several practice swings and he did the same. Loosening up the old muscles. All the while, he was conscious of Sophie's father looking at them through the window.

"Maybe we ought to go ahead without her," his father said, checking his watch for the umpteenth time. "She must've got held up in traffic. . . ."

"All right." He was pleased. He and his father could drive balls to their heart's content without Joy giving them instructions on the right way to do it.

They got a bucket of balls and started in. "The blind

leading the blind," his father joked. "Watch me, Tim." His father's feet rooted around in the grass, seeking the perfect stance. Elbows in, keep your eye on the ball. It looked so simple. Still, Tim got off a couple of good swings, and the feel and sound of the club hitting the ball just right was exhilarating. When you got it just so, you knew it.

"Not bad, fellas." Len Feeley stood behind them and, as they reached the bottom of the bucket, he came forward. "Where's the lady? You guys on your own today?"

"She'll be along," his father said. He knew his father didn't like Len, could tell by the stiff way his father spoke.

"What say, Tim? You want to buy another bucket? We both seem to be doing pretty well today."

"Any amount of balls you want, we got 'em. I might even throw in a couple extra, you fellas are such good customers."

"That isn't necessary," his father said. "You're in this to make money, after all."

Obviously, Len had something on his mind. He puffed ferociously on a cigarette. "I try to give these things up, they're killing me, and then I get hit with the latest. My wife says I oughta get outa the business, into something less stressful. I can't handle these things. What with one thing and another, my nerves are shot."

141

"That so?" His father handed him a new tee. "This one's for luck, Tim."

"My kid's getting these sicko letters in the mail," Len confided. Tim felt himself blush and quickly knelt to tie his sneaker, afraid his face might give him away.

"It's enough to drive me outa my skull." Len let another cigarette from the one he held. "I call the police; they give me the nothing-we-can-do routine. The guy's a crazy is what I say. Lock him up before he kills somebody. Like he's the kind puts razor blades in kids' Halloween candy, you know?"

Tim stuck the tee in the ground, and his hands trembled so hard he had difficulty lining up the ball. His father, always a polite man, paused to listen to what Len had to say.

Len dropped the cigarette on the ground and stomped on it, grinding it in with his heel. "See that? That's what I'd like to do to this pervert." The three of them stared down at Len's size-ten-EE suede loafer, complete with fancy brass buckle, as if fascinated by it. Taking out his handkerchief, Len bent and tenderly dusted off the buckle before resuming his complaint.

"What exactly do these letters say?" his father asked. "Are they threatening or what?"

"Threatening? Threatening! The guy's sick is what they are. The creep's always talking about souls and death, and mentioning parts of the body and all." Len's face flamed with emotion. By an enormous effort, Tim maintained a look of detached interest. His father shook his head slowly, sympathizing with Len's plight as the father of a girl who inspired such tawdry prurience.

"That's a shame," his father said. "I feel for you."

"My wife says I should cool it, not let it get to me," Len went on. "She says they're only cuckoo love letters, the guy means no harm, she says. And I tell her cuckoo love letters are dangerous. What does she know? The guy's a weirdo and he oughta be pulled off the street and locked up. I say they should book him on charges of harassment, if not downright obscenity." Len's little eyes glittered as he hauled out his handkerchief and dabbed at his moist face.

"I ask you, as a father, what would you do?" Len said. And, although the question was directed at his father, Len's eyes were trained on Tim.

His father said, "I guess just what you've done. If the police don't take the letters seriously, well, I guess you have to warn your daughter about speaking to strangers, taking rides from people she doesn't know, that sort of thing. How old is she?"

"She's fifteen, old enough to know better. I asked her did she know anybody might be writing this garbage to her and she says no, she doesn't know anybody would do that. I tell you, kids these days are no damn good. The lot of 'em. When we were kids, we just did pranks. You know, not bad stuff, just pranks. Like we'd let the air out of tires, steal apples off the neighbor's trees, pour sugar in somebody's gas tank if we didn't like what he said, stuff like that. All good, clean fun. Today, if they're not in jail by the time they're fourteen, you figure you got it made. I tell you, the world's going to hell in a handbasket."

"Hello, you two!" It was the first, indeed the only time he'd ever been glad to see Joy.

Len wiped his face one last time. "Sorry, folks. Didn't mean to get going like that. But I'm not myself. I'm so upset by this letter thing. But mark my words." Len's eyes were like two raisins in a rice pudding. "This guy's dangerous. The kind packs a BB gun so's he can shoot out streetlights, the kind lays in wait to mug old ladies walking on their canes."

Joy looked from him to his father, then at Len. "What's all this about?" she asked brightly.

Len was not quite finished. Leaning close, he whispered, "I think the guy obviously has sexual problems."

It was his father's turn to take out a handkerchief and wipe his brow. "I certainly hope you're wrong on that score," his father said.

A heavy silence fell.

Into it, Joy spoke, "You boys ready to hit a few

balls?" she said, jovial as any department-store Santa. "How about you, Tim? You want to start?"

Carefully, painstakingly, he set up his ball, nestling it neatly into the tee. Then he bent his knees, tucked in his elbows, placed his feet just so, kept his eye on the ball, and whiffed.

Chapter 19

"Do you feel all right, Tim?"

"Sure, Ma. Just a little queasy. Must've been those four hot dogs and three cans of soda Dad bought me at the driving range." He felt as if he'd been kicked in the stomach by a donkey.

"Did something happen with Dad? Is that it?"

"Ma, please. It's nothing. Nothing happened with Dad." He had a rule: never discuss one parent with the other. It was a question of loyalty to both. "How'd the show go? You make a bundle?"

She lifted the palms of both hands and held them open, and empty. "Not so's you'd notice. The booth fee was seventy-five dollars and my total take for the day came close to that. But there's always tomorrow. . . ." She shook her head. "You wouldn't believe some of the junk they come up with at one of these shows, Tim. A lot of the dealers don't know the difference between trinkets and trash."

"Hey, that wouldn't be a bad name for a shop, TRINKETS AND TRASH."

"Sort of like telling it like it is, right?" his mother said.

What had he done so wrong? All he did was write some flowery love letters, copied from the world's best. So, what made that a criminal act? He couldn't get over Sophie's father and the things he'd said. He was shattered by this turn of events. Where do I go from here? he asked himself.

"Tim." His mother hesitated. "I hate to ask you this because I know you'd rather work outside, but I was wondering if you'd help me in the shop this summer. I'd pay you minimum wage, and free room and board go with the job, of course." She smiled at him weakly.

There went his plan to hike the Appalachian Trail with Patrick. How could he turn her down?

"Kev take off?" he asked.

"Yes. That's it for Kev, Tim. You were right."

He patted her on the shoulder, comforting her as best he could, knowing what it must have cost her to say that. "Sure, Ma, I'll give you a hand. I don't know squat about antiques, but I guess I can learn."

"Oh, Tim, I'd be so grateful. You know as much as lots of people who call themselves experts. You can learn. I'll try to find some little old lady to tend the shop on weekends if I have to go to an auction to buy things. We'll close the shop two days a week, so you'll get a chance to have some fun. Thank you, Tim."

When he told Patrick about this turn of events, Patrick said, "Tough beans. But my father said he didn't want me hiking on the Appalachian Trail this summer. What he has in mind for me," Patrick said, fluttering his eyes to indicate despair, "is yard work. In his yard. For which he proposes to pay me peasant's wages and, in my spare time, which said father estimates at half an hour on Saturdays and time off for good behavior after church on Sundays, I am to be allowed to bask in the sun reading good books and resting up my muscles for the week ahead. Melissa's going to camp, so it's going to be me and my parents against the world."

"Woe is you," he said, secretly pleased that Patrick was in the same boat he was. "And woe also is me. I'm in the antique business with my mother, pushing porcelain and distressed armoires."

"One of the troubles with being sixteen," Patrick told him with a long face, "is that you're neither fish nor fowl. They tell you you're almost a man, but they still have that tight grip on you, telling you what you can do and what you can't. They get you out of Pampers, and you think you can lock them up in the closet if they get out of line. Next thing you know you're in bondage to them at minimum wage. I thought when I hit the big one-six I'd have it made. My troubles would be over. Now I know they're just beginning."

"You know something?" he said. "I'm always reading about these sixteen-year-old hotshots who invent a computer chip or a new use for the laser beam, and they get to be millionaires by the time they're seventeen. How come I never run into any of those guys? Where do you suppose they're all hiding?"

"On the Côte d'Azur, probably. Going skinny dipping with starlets at the Cannes Film Festival. Trouble with being a genius, a rich genius, Tim, is they're all burned out by the time they hit twenty. They've seen it all. What fun is that? Wouldn't you rather be an average jerk and have some fun?"

Talking to Patrick always made him feel better, if only for the nonce. He wanted to tell Patrick about Sophie and the love letters and Len Feeley's reaction, but he was ashamed and humiliated, and wasn't ready to share his humiliation yet. Not even with Patrick.

As if reading his thoughts, Patrick said, "How are

149

you doing with Sophie? Hit her up for a fast game of spin the bottle yet?"

He shrugged. "The status is about quo."

"Trouble with you, Tim, is you don't assert yourself. You have to pursue her. Go after her, let her know you think she's hotsy totsy, ask her out." Patrick snapped his fingers. "How about if we double date? That way, if she won't talk to you, you can talk to me and my date."

"What's her name?"

"It just so happens I met this girl," said Patrick, grinning. "Her name is Faith."

"As in Hope and Charity?"

"Yeah, those are her sisters, Hope and Charity. Anyway, she's really dishy, long blond hair, brown eyes, and built!" Patrick staggered, clutching his chest to illustrate his point. "I'm thinking of having a slumber party and asking her. No, I'm only kidding. I'm going to ask her if she wants to play pool. So, why don't you ask Sophie?"

"Sophie's into music. I'm not sure she plays pool," he said.

"Just ask. She can't kill you for asking, can she?"

He said OK, he'd ask her. So what am I supposed to do? he asked himself that night, lying in bed, looking up at the ceiling. Go up to her in the hall and say how about a game of pool Saturday night? No, it wouldn't work. But he'd give it a try.

On Monday he lay in wait for Sophie outside the science lab. He'd rehearsed what he'd say. "Hi, Sophie." Very upbeat. "How about a game of pool at my friend Patrick's house on Saturday night. I'll pick you up about eight, OK?"

It sounded simple, had sounded good alone in his room, mouthing the words, trying on his repertoire of facial expressions in front of the mirror, choosing just the right one. One of friendly interest—nothing serious, nothing to worry about. A boy asking a girl for a pool date. Don't bring your bathing suit, honey, it's not that kind of pool.

The bell rang, signifying the end of classes. His muscles knotted in anticipation. He felt her presence before he saw her. She came up on him, her little cat feet silent in their sneakers, long-legged, glossy-haired, carrying a pile of books across her chest like a breastplate. He turned and they looked into each other's eyes. It was the way he'd dreamed it would be. He smiled. She licked her lips so they shone redly.

"Hello, Sophie," he said softly, stepping toward her. She stepped back and away, a shy, virginal temptress, glorious in her confusion.

"Why don't you just knock it off!" Sophie hissed, small beads of spittle escaping from her mouth. "I know it's you. Barbara said so, and I know she's right. I'm telling my father if you keep it up. I can't stand it. You give me the creeps. Just knock it off, all right? Else I'll tell my father and he'll sick his Doberman on you. You're weird, really weird, you know that? You're sick. You need professional help. My father says whoever writes those letters to me is a sicko, and he's right. You are a sicko. And you know something?" Perspiration dotted her forehead, her upper lip. "You make me sicko, too."

He opened his mouth and was unable to speak. His hand shot out to grab her, to give her the sign of peace once more.

"Listen, Sophie," he croaked, "hear me out. Let me explain." She lunged out of reach.

"Don't touch me," she said in a calm, quiet voice that was worse than anger.

I meant no harm. Please, please Sophie, I adore you. Please, Sophie, give me a break.

Then she was gone, leaving in her wake the scent of cinnamon candy.

He turned and ran. The hall was crowded and plenty saw him go.

"What's wrong?" someone asked.

"Some guy's off his nut, I guess. Either that or the draft board's got his number."

He ran until his side ached. Bile rose in his throat

and filled his mouth. It was no good. He had given it his best shot. Sophie hated him. He could hardly breathe. He threw himself on the ground and rested his head in the dusty grass, which stank of dog droppings. And tried to think of nothing.

Chapter 20

It was a while before he could bear to think of Sophie's face, of the cruelty in it as she'd hurled words at him, words like pellets filled with poison. He kept his head down as he walked, imagining people looking at him peculiarly, as if asking themselves, "Who is this monster, this dealer in pornography?" He imagined Sophie screaming insults at him in his dreams. He caught his mother giving him sympathetic looks, as if someone he loved had died. Which, in a way, was what had happened.

"What happened?" Patrick asked at last. "I heard you and Sophie were mixing it up in the hall. They said she was really letting you have it with both barrels. I didn't know you knew her that well, Tim. Maybe if you tell me about it, I can help."

There was no sense keeping it to himself any longer. He told Patrick the whole story—the letters he'd copied from the book his mother had provided, the romantic impulse that had led him to it, the way he'd got caught up in it, listening to Len Feeley sound off at the driving range, and the confrontation with Sophie that had brought everything to a head.

Throughout, Patrick maintained a subdued silence, broken only by long, low whistles and general expressions of astonishment.

Finally, exhausted by his flow of words, he reached the end. He felt old, old and worn out. Not caring anymore what happened.

"I'm sorry, Tim. That's rough, really rough. Wish I could figure out something to make it better," Patrick said.

"Nothing can do that," he said. "I wish I was dead."

"Baloney." Patrick scowled. "Don't be an ass. You don't wish that. She's only a girl. Besides, she's not worth it, Tim. If she knew you, she'd think you were a good guy. She ought to talk to my mother. My mother'd tell her a thing or two about you."

"Yeah," he said, "same with my mother. I'm very big with mothers. It's only with the chicks I'm a washout. I'm just glad school's almost over. At least I won't have to face all those kids. I'm planning to work my tail off this summer, about twenty hours a day. After

155

I finish up at the antique shop, I'm going to mow lawns, clip hedges, dig wells, if necessary. I'm making plenty of bucks. Then I might go hiking on the Appalachian Trail by myself. If your father says you can't go . . ."

"Listen, someday we'll get a good laugh out of this, Tim. We'll tell our grandchildren about it. And we'll roll on the floor while we tell it. You wait."

"Thanks, Patrick. I appreciate your help. I hope you're right. Now I have to go help my mother move some gigantic pictures and tables and junk she bought at some tag sale. She's going crazy buying stuff."

"Did you tell her what happened?" Patrick wanted to know.

"Not yet. Maybe never. I haven't decided."

"I'll bet it would help if you did, Tim. She's probably wondering anyway, with you so down and all."

"Yeah. She thinks I might have a low-grade virus. When all else fails, a low-grade virus fills the bill, right? I'll see you, Patrick."

Patrick was a good friend. At least he had one good friend. His father called during the week. "How about this Saturday, Tim?" he said. "You up for some golf?"

"No thanks, Dad." He saw Len Feeley's outraged expression as he recounted the tale of the letters, saw his angry face as he recited further atrocities committed against his daughter.

"I'm helping Mom out. She's beefing up her business for the summer trade."

"Oh, Kev's not around?" His father's voice was casual.

"I guess he's off on vacation or something." His was equally casual. "I'll tell you what, though, Dad. If you want to play some tennis, I might see my way clear. I feel the need of some strenuous exercise. Tennis might be just the thing."

"Tennis it is, Tim. I'll call you later in the week to set up a time, after I see when the court's available." They played at the high-school courts, which were rented out by the hour.

His mother and father were involved in their own lives, and he, the carefree teenager, the vagabond adventurer, was hanging around, limp as a dirty sock. Ironic.

One torrid day in early July, the monsters' mother called. He recognized her voice immediately.

"Is that you, Tim?" she asked.

"No." He let his voice soar into an upper register. "Tim's gone. He left with his backpack and his hiking boots, so I don't expect him home for a long time. He might not be back until school begins."

"Oh." He could hear screams and grunts in the background, the sound of flesh against flesh. The monsters were playing a game, probably Monopoly.

"Children, please be good," the monsters' mother said in a pleading voice. "You wouldn't know of anyone who baby-sits, would you? It would only be for an hour or two. I simply have to get away by myself for a while." The mother's voice, ever patient, was showing signs of wear and tear.

"Nope. But if you leave your name and number, maybe I'll think of somebody." It crossed his mind to suggest Sophie. It would be a suitable punishment, but Sophie had sat once and never would again.

He went out to lie in the hammock with the Sunday funnies. His mother was having a wine-and-cheese bash at the shop, hoping to entice some new customers. Several of her friends were helping out. He'd begged off.

A soft breeze lulled him. He fell into a doze. No matter how tough his day had been, and he made sure his days were filled with hard work, he found himself waking sometime before the dawn and thinking about Sophie. He found himself hating her and tried not to. It wasn't her fault if she'd gotten the wrong idea. Anyone might've, he supposed. It was understandable. He looked like a weirdo, indeed had bent all his efforts toward that end—ergo, he was a weirdo. Never mind that underneath he was soft as a grape, loved his parents, dogs, and small children. He tried to view

158

himself dispassionately, see himself as Sophie had seen him. So he wrote love letters, love letters written a hundred years ago and good enough to be put in a book of the world's best. Boy, what did she want? He made a vow: never again would he write another love letter. He would conduct any romance, friendship, or momentary aberration by telephone. Or by smoke signals. His mother's stamps would remain untouched, his handwriting, used only for school assignments, would deteriorate to the point of complete illegibility. And no one would notice or care.

His soul, too, had taken a beating. No more flickering laser-beam light to it. It was flattened, battered, wasting away inside. Tough. He and it were wounded, beyond belief.

One night he and Patrick decided to go out to the Mall. It was Friday and his mother was out for dinner with some friends. Patrick's father would've been glad to drive them there, but that smacked too much of childhood. They hitched a ride with a big, beefy blond guy reeking of some exotic, long-lasting after-shave.

"You kids on the prowl, huh?" the beefy guy asked, grinning ear to ear. "When I was your age, boy, you couldn't tie me down on Fridays, Saturdays, Sundays either. Two beauties like yourselves must have the girls crawling all over, huh?" They knew that the beefy guy knew they didn't have girls all over them but they nodded, grinning back in what they hoped was a lascivious manner. The guy told them some dirty jokes, and they nudged each other and chortled, and by the time they got where they were going, their faces were stiff and stretched from all the grinning they'd had to do in return for the free ride.

"Good hunting!" shouted the beefy blond guy as they got out. A bunch of girls, standing huddled around a window display of bathing suits, turned languidly in their direction. He saw her at once. She stood at the far right, her friend Barbara beside her. She didn't look at him. He suspected she couldn't bring herself to look directly at him. Her eyes shifted rapidly from one spot to another, avoiding his. Her face was less lovely, less appealing than he'd remembered. It seemed she'd tricked him into thinking she was someone she was not. Or perhaps he'd fooled himself. It didn't matter. His heart stopped very briefly; then, to his astonishment, he was flooded with such a rush of overwhelming dislike he was stunned. Barbara giggled and shoved Sophie to make sure she wouldn't miss him. He made himself walk slowly to where the girls stood.

"Sophie," he said, and was surprised his voice sounded so normal, "you didn't have to do that. You didn't have to make a scene, let everybody in on it. I didn't mean any harm. It was just something I thought was a good idea. To copy the letters. They were written by famous people. They weren't mine. I wish they had been. I wanted you to know how I felt about you. It seemed a good way. I'm sorry. It was dumb. I should've known better."

Startled, Sophie didn't answer, though her mouth dropped open. He looked at Barbara. Her eyes were like hatpins—small, sharp, and cold. Shiny eyes with no light shining from them.

"It's all right, Sophie. I won't write to you again. I don't feel anything for you anymore. You don't have to worry."

He turned and walked away. Out of sight of them, he leaned against a wall, breathing hard.

Patrick appeared. "I'm proud of you, Tim," Patrick said. "That took a lot of guts. You deserve a medal. That was really fine. You finished her off but good."

"Yeah," he said. "I did, didn't I?"

But, as he spoke, there were tears in his eyes.

Chapter 21

The next couple of weeks were plenty gloomy. To cheer himself up, he took to wearing an old rubber Richard Nixon mask around the house. The first time he wore the mask, his mother screamed and backed into a corner. His father had worn the mask to a New Year's Eve party at the height of Watergate. Now his father, once choleric at the mention of Nixon's name, no longer cared. The fun, he said, had gone out of politics.

He considered wearing the mask when he rode out to the Collinses' to mow their lawn. His mother said it was too dangerous—someone might take a potshot at him. He said how about wearing his headphones instead? Too dangerous, his mother said. He wouldn't be able to hear someone honking at him, telling him to get out of the way.

Mr. Collins had a ride-'em mower, a second hand job that looked as if it might be the first ride-'em ever invented. Mrs. Collins fed him lemonade and brownies made from a mix, before and after the mowing. Mr. Collins paid him the same amount he would've if he'd had a push mower. The Collinses' daughter Marilou, fifteen and nubile, had a slight squint and enormous feet and read poetry and played chess when she wasn't making goo-goo eyes at him. Which should've restored his confidence and didn't.

Summer, which had always been his favorite time, dragged. Patrick went to Florida to visit his grandfather. "The temperature's hit over a hundred every day for a week," Patrick said gloomily. "Disney World, here I come. I'm too old for it, but maybe I'll get to shake hands with Donald Duck."

He ran into Tony Montaldo in the supermarket.

"My mother might have to take me to an orthodontist," Tony said. "My teeth are killing me. If I need surgery, it's gonna cost you big bucks, King Kong. Know what? My father said he never would've taken you for a violent guy. He was amazed when I told him it was you who did it to me. Absolutely amazed."

"Me, too," he said. "Ordinarily, I'm a peace lover. But you asked for it, and I'd do it again. You tried my soul once too often, kid."

163

He dreamed he was dancing to wild music, totally out of control. His partner's hair kept getting in his eyes, so he couldn't see who she was. Melissa stood on the sidelines, mouthing words, trying to tell him something.

If there'd been another way of handling Tony, he'd have taken it. But sometimes, he reflected, a good punch in the nose is worth a hundred soft words.

He did not, would not, allow himself to think of Sophie.

That night he and his mother went out for dinner to celebrate. She'd made her first real money, sold a lot of old linens to a collector who'd paid her three times what the linens had cost her.

She was jubilant. "I think I've finally made the big breakthrough, Tim," she said, eyes sparkling, "I feel it in my bones. And I have you to thank for part of it. If you hadn't been such a big help this summer, I don't think I could've done it."

"Anytime, Ma. You could've done it on your own, though." He took pride in the knowledge that he had been of some help to her. It made him feel good, and not many things did lately. "What looks good for dessert?"

The restaurant was famous for its wide choice of excellent desserts. He had about narrowed it down to either the apple pie à la mode or the profiterole with hot chocolate sauce when his mother said, "Who is that girl over there, Tim? She keeps looking over here as if she knows you."

It was Sophie. Who, when she saw him looking at her, had the grace to duck down behind her menu, where she stayed until he turned away.

"Yeah, it's a girl who used to sit for the monsters. A girl I knew in school. I think I'll have the profiterole. How about you?" and that was that. He'd never told his mother about Sophie. It was still too hurtful to talk about. The time had never seemed ripe. Someday he would be able to talk about it with ease. But that day was far away. Until then, Sophie was someone he'd once known, and not well, at that.

Inside him, a small spot ached dully, like a tooth that was giving trouble and probably would give more. Only he couldn't bite down on his aching spot, to ease, even momentarily, the pain. It would have to heal itself. He stole another glance at Sophie on his way out of the restaurant and felt only a curious detachment, a sense of wonder that he had spent so much time and effort trying to win her heart as well as her attention. Just as well he hadn't succeeded. If he'd gotten to know her better, he probably wouldn't have liked her nearly as well as he imagined. That was life. He'd know better next time.

Chapter 22

The shoemaker's children go barefoot. And the lawn mower's lawn grows long and thick and studded with weeds because the lawn mower is out mowing other people's lawns.

His mother said she'd pay him for mowing their lawn, but he said nix. That would be chintzy, to take money for mowing his own lawn.

The mower wouldn't start. He pulled at it repeatedly, and it refused to fire. He wondered if he could talk his mother into buying a ride-'em number, and grinned, thinking of his father's face if he caught him mowing the lawn sitting down. It went against the old work ethic. Honest toil demanded honest sweat and nothing else would do.

"Benjy!" cried a new and different voice. So the

monsters' mother had found herself a sitter after all. God bless her. The sitter and the mother. They both deserved medals. He peered out from behind his phony glasses and his bangs, which had been let go, much like the lawn, and were badly in need of trimming. He saw the monsters milling around the screen door, which was still pockmarked with holes large enough to admit a whole fleet of mosquitoes. The sitter must've lured them there with some irresistible bait. Maybe half a steer, done rare, or a bulging bag of M&M's. Whatever, he wished her well. The monsters, from a distance, seemed to have grown like the proverbial weeds. He wished the new sitter would be big and strong and wily. And fast on her feet.

The mower started up at last. His father would've been proud. Sweat poured down his face. He took off his glasses, as they only made things worse. He found an oily rag in the garage, which he tore into strips to make a proper sweatband for himself. Perfect. He caught a glimpse of himself in the garage window, bringing to mind John McEnroe at Wimbledon or, better still, Rambo returning from the wars. Either way, the sweatband lent him an air of dissolution, which he found rather sexy and hoped others might find sexy, too.

No matter how hard he worked, he made only a slight dent in the lawn's raggle-taggle appearance.

Pausing to rest, he saw a tall woman over at the monsters' house. She wore a white hat and seemed to be telling them something. And they seemed to be listening. A first. Perhaps she was a witch. A witch in a white hat would be a switch. Maybe her rates were higher than your average, everyday baby-sitter, but she was worth every penny. More power to her. Cast that spell, baby, he told her. I salute you. If he hadn't been so eager to finish the job, he might've crossed over to monster territory and introduced himself.

When at last he'd finished and the lawn resembled a greensward, he admired his work. And hoped his father might come over tonight, maybe for dinner, and see the good job he'd done. He had tried not to let his father's approval mean so much, but it did.

He'd just stepped out of the shower when he heard the telephone. Patrick said, "Where you been, fool? I've been ringing and ringing. I was about to call the cops."

"Hey, you're back. I was mowing the lawn. How was it?"

"Mickey and Minnie sent their best. Want to come over and shoot the breeze and some pool?"

"Sure. I'll be over as soon as I cut my hair."

"Hey, if things are that tough," Patrick said, "I'll lend you barber money."

"It's just in the front. My bangs are overrunning my forehead. Hang in. I'll be there in a trice."

He rode his bike over to Patrick's, hunched over the handlebars in a true racer's crouch, anxious to make time. He'd missed Patrick.

"I hope you did a better job on your lawn than you did on your hair," Patrick said when he opened the door. "Come on down. We have the joint to ourselves."

He hadn't improved his technique at pool, but then, neither had Patrick. They fooled around some, making like hustlers. Outside, the sun shone. Inside, all was cool depravity as they squinted out from under their green eyeshades, and pushed up their sleeves, and considered the possibilities of each shot.

"Did you run into any girls out there?" he asked Patrick.

"Only one worth talking about. Only trouble was"—Patrick went for the side pocket—"she couldn't shake these seven little nerds who followed her everywhere. 'Name's Snow White,' she said. 'What's yours?' So you know what I told her?"

Patrick missed his shot.

"I said, 'Call me Ishmael.' What's with you?" Patrick asked. "You had any romantic adventures since I've been gone?"

Tim took a long time setting up his next shot.

"Nope," he said. "I saw Sophie at a restaurant one night. She was looking at me, and when I looked back, she ducked behind her menu." His cue slipped and he wound up behind the eight ball. A place he was not unused to.

"She's embarrassed, that's why she hid," Patrick told him. "I wouldn't be surprised if she called you up one of these days to apologize for the way she acted."

He snorted. "If she did, I'd tell her I was out of town."

A tall woman came halfway down the stairs and bent over, looking at them. He started to say, "Hi, Mrs. Scanlon," but it wasn't Mrs. Scanlon. Maybe it was her sister.

"Hello," the woman said. Patrick never even looked at her, never acknowledged her presence. Maybe Patrick's mother had had a face-lift. It sure looked like her. He smiled at her tentatively.

"I'm Tim Owen," he said.

"Hello, Tim," she said, staying put.

"Get lost," said Patrick.

He was astonished at Patrick's bad manners. If Patrick's mother had been around, she would've let him have it.

"Why don't you just go bury your head in the sand, Melissa," Patrick said.

Melissa? *Melissa!*

Melissa came down several steps and stood there, smiling at him. "I saw you this afternoon, Tim," she said. "When you were mowing the lawn."

He was tongue-tied and web-footed, trying to piece things together. "That was you?" he said at last, in his usual brilliant manner. "Baby-sitting next door with the monsters?"

"They didn't give me a speck of trouble. All I did was read them a couple of Grimm's fairy tales. It was like waving a wand over them. They loved "Hansel and Gretel." You know that part where the witch fattens Hansel up so she can eat him? They thought that was really cool. Next thing I knew, they were trying to fit Benjy in the oven, which they'd turned on high, to roast him. I got to them just in time. Benjy wasn't even singed." Melissa's merry laugh rang out. "I'd heard those kids were a problem, but they were pussycats for me."

"Did they lock you in the bathroom?" he asked, curious. "They almost always lock their sitters in the bathroom."

"Well, they would've but I found the key under the rug and put it in my pocket for safekeeping. We got along fine," Melissa said.

"Tim, your shot." Patrick nudged him.

He bent over the table, brandishing his cue, pretending great interest in his next move. His head buzzed. What had happened to Melissa? He couldn't very well ask, "Hey, Melissa, what gives? Only a couple of months ago, you were fat and ugly. What happened?" She might take offense. Still, it was a valid question.

Upstairs the telephone rang, and Melissa thundered to answer.

"All of a sudden," Patrick said gloomily, "she's got 'em stacked up on the runway. Everywhere you turn, these dudes who wouldn't have looked at her cross-eyed are standing in line waiting for a turn to nuzzle Melissa. It's indecent. My mother and father are practically having a heart attack."

"Yeah." He took his chance. "I noticed she's changed some. What *did* happen to her?"

"For one thing, she turned fourteen," Patrick said, as if that explained the miracle. "For another, she dropped twenty-two pounds at the fat camp she went to. What with one thing and another, it's a puzzlement. I think my parents wish they'd left her the way she was. That way, nobody would look twice at her. But now the fat's in the fire, both literally and figuratively. Last night I heard my father tell my mother he thought sex was rearing its ugly head around here. And I don't think he meant me. Pretty racy talk from the old man, huh?"

Well put, Mr. Scanlon, he thought. Very well put. He hung around so long, hoping Melissa would return, that Mrs. Scanlon came down to announce dinner and asked him if he'd like to stay.

"Thanks," he said reluctantly, "but I can't. My father's coming over. I'll take a rain check, if it's all right with you."

Chapter 23

"So, the way it looks now," his father said, watching as his mother dished up the steak-and-kidney pie, "I'll be going out to the coast next week to try to line up an apartment. They want me there by the first of October."

"I think that's wonderful, Andrew. I'm very happy for you." His mother came around the table and kissed his father's cheek. "I'm thrilled at your getting such a wonderful promotion. I'll bet you'll love living in California, too."

"Well"—his father looked down at his plate hungrily—"my contract's good for two years. That's not long. If, at the end of that time, things haven't worked out for any reason, I can always come back. They're keeping a place open for me here, they told me."

"They must think very highly of you, Andrew. Here's to your great success." They raised their glasses and drank to his father, whose company, he had just told them, was sending him out to take over the management of a new plant they were building outside San Francisco.

"I hope you'll come visit me, Tim," his father said. "That's the only bad part about this—leaving you. And, of course, I'll miss you, too, Maddy. I'll miss you both."

"What about Joy? Is she going along?" One thing about his mother, if she wanted to know something, she asked the direct question. She never minced words.

"Joy's got herself a new beau." His father made small noises of pleasure at his mother's cooking, a habit that had endeared him to her early on.

"I'll bet the guy has a five handicap," Tim said. His father laughed. "He'd better have."

All in all, it had been an eventful day, he reflected, as he scraped the plates and listened to the rise and fall of his parents' voices. First Melissa's metamorphosis, then his father's announcement that he was moving to California. Two very big happenings. At last he had to admit something to himself, something he'd been wrestling with for some time. His mother and father were not going to get remarried. He had hoped they would, prayed it might happen. People did get remarried. He was always reading or hearing about people who did. But now he knew it would never happen to them. His mother and father both were happily embarked on new ventures. He was the only member of the family dragging his feet, flailing away at life, running in place.

The next day, Patrick's mother asked him if he'd come to a family cookout they were having at six. "I'd love to!" he shouted, trying vainly to conceal his enthusiasm. He took pains with his appearance, parting his hair on the left side, then on the right. Then he tried for the casual look, no part at all. He looked like a Neanderthal man fresh from the bush. On probation. A middle part was quaint. He looked like Alfalfa. Then he rummaged through his drawers for matching socks, having decided to spare no effort or expense to look suave. He settled for two pale-gray socks with red stripes.

Going all out, aren't you? he told his mirror image. His little voice, silenced for a while, shot back with "You're wasting your time, bud. You heard what Patrick said, she's got 'em stacked up on the runway."

But I saw her first, he answered back.

"Oh yeah?" The little voice was feeling testy.

"Wasn't it nice of Mrs. Scanlon to include you?" his mother said. "Is it a party?"

"I don't know. Patrick's back from Florida and Melissa's back from camp, so I guess it's a family reunion, sort of."

"Well, I think you won points with Mrs. Scanlon when you took Melissa to the tea dance." His mother fiddled with her lipstick. "That's the kind of thing the mother of an unattractive thirteen-year-old girl never forgets, Tim."

"Unattractive!" The word burst from him, unannounced. "You oughta see her now, Mom. She's something! She went to a fat camp and shed piles of pounds. Plus, she shed her zits and had her hair cut. She's got beautiful red hair. All the Scanlons have red hair, you know."

His mother turned to look at him. She was smiling. "Well, what do you know? Melissa must really be something. I've never heard you wax so enthusiastic about a girl before, Tim."

He'd gone too far.

"She's fourteen now," he said, backing off. "I guess when most girls hit fourteen, they sort of blossom. I've got to split, Ma. Mrs. Scanlon said six, and I'm running late."

"Have a good time, Timmy. Give the Scanlons my best." His mother still held her lipstick aloft, a bemused expression on her face.

A gibbous moon rose from behind a bank of clouds as the scent of hamburgers rose from the Scanlons' grill. Mr. Scanlon basted the burgers with his special sauce, the ingredients of which were top secret. Tim was the only guest.

It was tough going, keeping his eyes off Melissa. Every time he stole a peek, she was looking back. They sat down at the outdoor table, and the telephone rang.

"If that's for you, Missy"—Mr. Scanlon spoke, plainly irritated— "tell him you're about to have dinner and not to call back for an hour."

"And this is only the beginning," Mrs. Scanlon murmured.

"I thought only girls hung out on the phone so much," said Patrick. "Those cretins who keep calling Missy never got the word, apparently. Half of them haven't even gone through a change of voice yet. The other day, I answered, and I thought it was a girl until he said, 'Tell her George called.' George isn't even dry behind the ears."

"It wasn't so long ago," Mr. Scanlon reminded Patrick, "that the same might have been said about you. Age is relative, after all. A two-year-old thinks a six-year-old is old. And I used to think fifty was ancient, until I realized I would be fifty in three years and I'm still a broth of a boy. Another burger, Tim?"

"No thanks, Mr. Scanlon. I've had three already."

"Save room for dessert, Tim. It's coconut cake."

Mrs. Scanlon's coconut cake was so outstanding, the mere thought of it almost drove Melissa out of his mind. After supper, the whole crowd trooped down to the pool room. Melissa and her mother played against Patrick and Tim. He let Melissa win. That's what he told himself.

"I guess I'd better take off," he said, the chiming of the Scanlons' clock reminding him of the passage of time. Mr. Scanlon offered to run him home but he said he had his bicycle. He said good night and thank you very much and Melissa escorted him to the door.

"Well, guess I'll see you in high school come September, huh, Melissa?" he said. Sometimes his own dialogue almost put him to sleep. Imagine what it did to her. How come when he was alone he always managed to sound so dynamic, so positive, each word a pearl, but when he was with a girl, everything came out sounding stolid and heavy, like a politician discussing tax reform?

"My mother and father are making me go to the Academy up the river," Melissa said with a long face. "I want to go to the high school, but they're afraid I would get too boy crazy there. I wouldn't, but they think so."

"Oh." He was taken aback, wondering where to go from here.

"Tim, I was thinking," and although Melissa was

tall, almost as tall as he, she managed to give the effect of being petite as she glanced up at him through her eyelashes.

"Yeah?"

"If I write you, will you write back?" Melissa said in a rush.

"You mean we'd be correspondents, sort of," he said, his head in a muddle.

She nodded eagerly. "I think it would be fun. When I get my new address, I'll send it to you. How would that be?"

"Fine. Great." Melissa put out her hand and he took it and held it gingerly in his, stroking it gently, as if it was a baby rabbit just out of its mother's womb.

"Tim," Melissa breathed.

"Hey, you guys!" Patrick loomed. "I thought you'd gone, Tim."

He jumped away and assumed a devil-may-care look, which seemed to suit the occasion. "I was just telling Melissa about high school, on account of she's not going there," he said.

"Well," said Patrick, "I guess that's as good a reason to tell her about it as any."

"Missy!" Mr. Scanlon bellowed. "Telephone!"

Melissa raced to answer, and he departed at last, serenaded by Patrick singing one from his large store of golden oldies. The gibbous moon watched sourly as he pushed his bicycle out to the street and climbed aboard for the return trip.

The next morning, before he was completely awake, reason took hold and threw romance out on its ear.

"I'm not writing her any letters," he grumbled, as if someone had been trying to talk him into it. He punched his pillow savagely and thought, I'll call her up when the rates are down. After six P.M. and before eight A.M. But no more letters. Once burned, twice shy.

He tossed and turned, trying to get back to sleep. He gave his pillow a final thump and a book fell out.

One Hundred of the World's Best Love Letters stared him in the face. No sirree. Begone. Out, damned spot. Take off.

He couldn't resist flipping it open.

"My sweet lass!" caught his eye. "Is it possible I cannot have the satisfaction of weeping at the foot of your bed and kissing your beautiful hands?"

He imagined Melissa's face as she read the words.

It's a fool who doesn't learn from his mistakes, the little voice said, somewhat pompously.

Get lost, he told the little voice. What do you know?

Instead of throwing the book across the room, he tucked it carefully under his subdued pillow, and as he shut his eyes for forty more winks, a beatific smile wreathed his face.

About the Author

Constance C. Greene has been a writer for many years. Her first book for young people was published in 1969, and since then she has written nearly twenty books, many of them selected by the American Library Association as Notable Books. About THE LOVE LETTERS OF J. TIMOTHY OWEN, Ms. Greene writes, "It seemed to me that love letters had gone out of style, as had romanticism. I wrote the book to tell people that romantics still live."

She says her hobbies are playing golf, cooking, going to auctions, and "eavesdropping, a useful hobby for a writer." Constance C. Greene lives on Long Island with her husband. She has five grown children.